The L

Born in 1968, Fabrice Bourland lives in the Paris region. He has worked extensively as a book and magazine editor, and many of his own short stories have been published in French. He is the author of *The Baker Street Phantom*, also published by Gallic Books.

Morag Young lives in Kent and works as a translator. Her translations include *Checkout: A Life on the Tills* by Anna Sam and Fabrice Bourland's *The Baker Street Phantom*.

THE DREAM KILLER OF PARIS

THE DREAM KILLER
OF PARIS

FABRICE BOURLAND

Translated by Morag Young

Gallic Books

London

A Gallic Book

First published as *Les portes du sommeil* by Éditions 10/18
Copyright © Éditions 10/18, Département d'Univers Poche, 2008

First published in Great Britain in 2012 by Gallic Books,
59 Ebury Street, London SW1W 0NZ

A CIP record for this book is available from the British Library
ISBN 978-1-906040-32-1

Typeset in Fournier by Gallic Books
Printed and bound by CPI (SN14 6LH)

24681097531

My thanks to Geneviève and Jean
who gave me such a warm welcome at their inn

'Two gates of Sleep there are, whereof the one, they say, is horn and offers a ready exit to true shades, the other shining with the sheen of polished ivory, but delusive dreams issue upward through it from the world below.'
Virgil, *The Aeneid*, Book VI, translated by H. R. Fairclough

'Never have I been able to pass without a shudder through those gates of ivory or horn which divide us from the invisible world.'
Gérard de Nerval, *Aurélia*, Part I, chapter 1

'It may appear extraordinary but sleep is not only the most powerful state but also the most lucid one for thought.'
Charles Nodier, *Some Phenomena of Sleep*, 1831

CONTENTS

FOREWORD BY THE PUBLISHER

As readers may remember, we were sent the manuscript of The Baker Street Phantom[1], *Andrew Fowler Singleton's previous adventure, in the post and were so impressed that we decided to publish it as quickly as possible. Readers may also recall that William H. Barnett, son of John W. Barnett, the detective writer's executor, told us in his accompanying letter that there were several folders in his father's attic that might contain more unpublished stories.*

We immediately contacted him and he confirmed that twelve files had been found in a trunk and that these files did indeed contain unpublished manuscripts written by the celebrated detective. He had not yet had time to read them all but said he would be happy to send us the second adventure soon, a tale which, in his view, was just as disconcerting as the first.

A few days later we duly received a large envelope from Northampton containing 235 typed pages, carefully protected in a blue folder. On the first page was the title The Dream Killer of Paris *in capital letters.*

Naturally, we read the manuscript straight away. This time the adventure had taken Singleton, in October 1934, to Paris and its literary and spiritualist circles, as well as to Vienna. We must warn readers that, as in his previous tale, the facts appear to be highly implausible. And yet, as a result of a number of checks carried out over the past few weeks, in particular at the archives of the French police force and the Institut Métapsychique International, we can confirm that this account is an accurate reflection of events.

Unlike The Baker Street Phantom, *where it was difficult to determine when it had been written, in this instance a sentence in the epilogue (the* reference to the 'young man') seems to indicate that the manuscript was written between 1947 and 1950. As for the young man in question, our attempts to find him have been unsuccessful. We don't know therefore whether Auguste was eventually admitted to the Academy or not.

All things considered, this second document sheds a little more light on why the writer, and later his legal executor, wanted to keep some of his cases out of the public eye. In the stories we were already familiar with, bodies might disappear without explanation, castles be filled with ghosts, and evil creatures float in the air but, in the end, the real guilty parties always proved to be made of flesh and blood. It is probable that Andrew Fowler Singleton, mindful of his reputation, was reluctant to publish those cases which had led him to enter a realm outside conventional understanding. He knew that the excessive scepticism which poisons our age would make it impossible for these tales to be taken seriously.

And perhaps he was right – the incredulity already expressed by many readers of Phantom is the best proof of that.

Stanley Cartwright, 3 May 2007

I

FATA MORGANA

It had been an exceptionally warm year across most of Europe, and even in London, in Montague Street, temperatures were still high at the beginning of autumn. I recall that when my business partner James Trelawney and I, Andrew Fowler Singleton, brought the shameful activities of the 'gang of bell thieves' to an end in the last days of September, we were in shirtsleeves, our foreheads beaded with sweat. It had been a truly incredible case which had taken us the length and breadth of Great Britain for a number of weeks, from Swansea to Ipswich; from Edinburgh to the tip of Cornwall.

Consequently, on the morning of Tuesday, 16 October 1934, with no new cases in the offing in London, I decided to go to Paris. I wanted to spend a few days trying to solve a particular mystery that I had put off for far too long.

As I was packing my travelling bag with a few essentials, James's athletic form appeared in the sitting-room doorway – he had just dragged himself out of bed. I'd put my plan to him on numerous occasions but each time he'd merely looked doubtful. At that moment he was pondering the reason for my haste.

'Still obsessed by the death of Gérard de Nerval?' he asked, smoothing a recalcitrant lock of blond hair on top of his head. 'For goodness' sake, the man killed himself seventy years ago, Andrew! What on earth are you hoping to find out?'

'I came across some disturbing information in this book,' I replied, as I tried to push a biography of the poet[2] acquired a few days earlier in a French bookshop in Kensington into my bag, alongside six volumes of his complete works published by Honoré Champion. 'There are too many different versions of the discovery of his body in Rue de la Vieille-Lanterne. And the number of medical checks carried out in the morgue afterwards seems very high for a simple case of suicide by hanging.'

'You told me yourself that his friends were famous writers. It's hardly surprising that they discussed the circumstances of his death, with each one having his own theory. And even if Nerval didn't commit suicide, it just means that he was killed for a few pennies by a local villain. Does it really make any difference? Do you think you'll find one of the murderer's family and force a confession out of him?'

'I don't claim to be rewriting history. I just want to find answers to some questions that fascinate me. Now, James, are you going to tell me if you're coming or not?'

'It's just such a waste of time,' my partner replied, yawning so widely that I thought he'd break his jaw. 'My programme's all mapped out: swimming, cricket and the pictures. It's so nice not having anything to do! Afterwards, well, I'll keep my strength up with that wonderful calf's sweetbread they serve at McInnes's, washed down with a pint, and then I'll go and forget my sorrows in the arms of a pretty girl. In a week or so, if you still want to fritter your time away on the other side of the Channel and if no damsel has decided to cross the threshold of this flat to ask for my assistance, then maybe I'll join you.'

'Bah! You'll show up within a week – I'm willing to bet on it!'

'Very well, I bet you a case of Vouvray. But I beg you, Andrew: if an interesting case does turn up, don't let it slip through your fingers because you had your head buried in a book. You will let me know, won't you?'

'I promise,' I replied, putting on my jacket. 'But let's make it two cases of wine. I'll wire you the address of my hotel as soon as I get there.'

We embraced, laughing like children, and I left the home of Miss Sigwarth, our wonderful landlady. We had been renting rooms on the first floor for two years and, although our means had improved substantially, allowing us to take a more spacious flat, we were reluctant to leave the old lady.

Seeing no taxis in Montague Street, I walked to the rank in Great Russell Street, a hundred yards away, where I found a cab which dropped me outside Victoria station in no time.

At the Southern Railway ticket studyI paid the twenty-pound fare for the journey (a tidy sum but it's not every day that you travel on one of the world's most luxurious trains) and on the stroke of eleven, in keeping with its reputation for punctuality, the Golden Arrow moved off.

At half past twelve I was in Dover. Ah, the miracle of human ingenuity! Had I had the choice, I would willingly have swapped my easy existence in this crowded century for the life of a young knight in the time of the houses of York and Lancaster, or that of a trapper on the prairies of the Wild West, or an explorer in the South Seas, or a romantic young blade under the July monarchy in France. Nonetheless, I admit that travelling from the hustle and bustle of Soho to the excitement of the Latin Quarter in just a few hours was a privilege for which I was grateful to the modern world.

This was not the first time I had made the journey from London to Paris since James and I had set ourselves up in the English capital. Thanks to the success of our first cases, our reputation had spread to the Continent and on three occasions we had helped the Paris police: firstly, to solve the case of the Phantom Violin at the end of August 1932; then during the unlikely affair of the Curse of the Fresnoys, as the press referred to it in their excessive coverage, which had the public on tenterhooks for many weeks; and finally, in the case of the Cut-throat with the Broken Watch, which lingered in the memories of all at the Eclipse studios in Billancourt. But on those trips I had never had time to stroll through the streets of Paris, the city I had dreamt about for as long as I can remember.

I was sixteen when I first read Gérard de Nerval and, as a sensitive and tormented young man, I had immediately recognised the writer as a kindred spirit. It was while I was at boarding school in Dartmouth, Nova Scotia (the province where I was born), during a French lesson. I was reading his poems 'El Desdichado' and 'Fantaisie'. Accompanying them was a short biography which briefly recounted the time the author had spent in a mental asylum and, above all, his tragic end. On the night of 25 January 1855, Nerval, then aged forty-six, had hanged himself from a grating in Rue de la Vieille-Lanterne in one of the most sordid areas of the city. Some had suspected foul play but that theory had quickly been discounted. The police investigation concluded that it was suicide.

Since my time at boarding school, I had often returned to Nerval's work, always with the same fervour. I'd found out about his life and read most of the articles written about him, although, after leaving my father's house, these had proved very difficult to get hold of in America and England. I'd always promised myself that one day I would investigate the mystery surrounding his death. Had he hanged himself one night in despair or had it been a cowardly murder?

At quarter to one I boarded the *Canterbury*, an imposing steamer chartered by the Southern Railway and the Compagnie du Nord, enabling passengers to cross the Channel in record time. In less than five hours, after being whisked to my destination on board the *Flèche d'Or*, the Golden Arrow's French alter ego, I would be walking upon the cobblestones of the City of Light!

In the meantime, I intended to make the most of the crossing.

Stretched out on a deckchair, with my body facing east and my face caressed by spray and soft sunlight, I reread some pages from *Sylvie*. The English coastline had already disappeared over the horizon and the French coast, from Calais to several miles beyond the lighthouse at Cap Gris-Nez, was only just becoming visible. Suddenly, as I was about to nod off, I stared wide-eyed at a staggering vision. Fairly high above the horizon, to the right of the Boulogne coastline, and therefore directly above the glittering water of the Channel, was an immense dream-like landscape that went on for about a mile and created the illusion of a long valley in green and orange tones, covered in vines and densely wooded. I could see, scattered here and there on steep hillsides, the roofs and steeples of mythical towns peeping through the foliage of conifers and chestnut trees. Snaking through the middle of this panorama that had sprung from nowhere was a blue river as wide as the Thames, with what appeared to be paddle steamers plying its fast-flowing waters. Near the banks, solemn rocky peaks were shrouded in mist and, at the top, I could see the shadowy forms of medieval castles or small ruined forts. One of the castles in particular, which overlooked the river opposite a small island, commanded my attention: it was an eyrie composed of a tall square tower and another lower one with a pointed roof.

What was this vision? Had I fallen into a rapturous sleep without realising it? Or was I fully aware of what was going on around me and witnessing one of those incredible mirages which are sometimes depicted in tales of expeditions to distant lands?

'*Fata Morgana!*' said a soft female voice nearby.

'*Fata Morgana!*' I repeated, astounded. I turned to the person who had spoken.

In the deckchair to my right (which I could have sworn had been empty a few moments before) was a young woman with a grace as miraculous as the vision I had just witnessed. She was about twenty and impeccably dressed in a long white silk tunic. Barefoot, with a mane of soft blond hair falling over her shoulders, she continued to study the distant phenomenon. I, for my part, had almost forgotten its existence, so difficult was it for me to turn away from a profile worthy of the statues of Antiquity.

'Do you believe in mirages?' she asked, leaning towards me, her expression candid, her dark eyes sparkling like two uncut gems.

'Well …'

Deep down, I had the indefinable impression that I was experiencing something unique, almost supernatural. The fantastic spectacle in the sky, this mysterious stranger next to me, the intoxicating heat running through my veins, the distant buzzing in my ears …

'Well, we're seeing the same thing,' I continued. 'So the mirage must exist, there's no doubt about it.'

Just then I discovered that I could tear my eyes away from the young woman's face, as if she had suddenly released me from her spell. On the horizon, the suspended valley was already beginning to disintegrate and gradually metamorphose into a trail of iridescent clouds. In a few moments there would be no trace of it.

We observed this slow transformation in respectful silence until it was complete. Then, fearing above all that the female vision at my side would disappear as quickly as the celestial one, I tried to hold on to her by steering the conversation towards a more down-to-earth subject.

'My name is Singleton, Andrew Fowler Singleton. It's a—'

'You misunderstood me, Mr Singleton. I asked you if you believed in *fata Morgana*, in the possibility that what we have seen has some kind of meaning.'

'All I know is that it was an atmospheric phenomenon,' I replied, both amused by and surprised at her insistence. 'I know it's traditionally linked to Morgan le Fay, hence the name, and that the fairy created mirages from Etna, which captivated the people of the Bay of Naples and the residents of Reggio Calabria in the Straits of Messina. They were eager to see portents in these mirages. But I've never seen one before and, what's more, I didn't know that such an illusion could be produced in the northern waters of the Channel.'

'I think the people you mention are absolutely right. I'm certain it contains a hidden meaning.'

'And what might that be?'

'Do you dream, Mr Singleton?'

'Yes, very often.'

'Wonderful! Apparently, there are people who never dream.'

'They don't remember, that's all. Everyone dreams; you can't help it.'

'I don't mean that kind of dream. Do you have *real dreams* that you can still smell when you wake up, which follow you around throughout the day and which, sometimes, go on for several nights? Dreams which transform you, shape you, improve you?'

'Ah! If you mean that kind of dream, then no, I must say that I've never had one like that.'

'You will, you will. But let me give you a piece of advice. When it happens, don't forget to write it down so that it may influence your waking hours.'

'I will. But, about the mirage we've just seen together – and sorry to press the point – what is the hidden meaning you mentioned earlier?'

'Oh, I couldn't tell you! All I can say is that it was a message.'

'A message? Sent by whom?'

'Elemental spirits! Sylphs, gnomes, nymphs, salamanders ...'

Her answer left me deeply perplexed. What did she mean? Was she making fun of me?

The steamer's foghorn suddenly brought me back to reality. My gaze was irresistibly drawn to the area of the sky where, not so long ago, I had thought I'd seen a majestic landscape. A flight of cormorants now took its place.

I turned to my companion but the ochre and blue chair was empty.

Where had she gone? I scoured the deck in every direction but couldn't see her golden mane anywhere.

In Calais at the harbour station and later in the Pullman carriages of the *Flèche d'Or* I looked for her again among the passengers – in vain. It was as if she had disappeared into thin air and I thought it unlikely I would ever see her again.

As the train sped through the French countryside at more than seventy miles an hour, I considered the strange meeting again. By the time the train had stopped at Platform 1 of the Gare du Nord, my memory of the scene had become so uncertain that I wondered if I hadn't imagined the whole thing. Indeed, what if, after all, the young woman herself was a mirage. *Fata Morgana!*

II

TOUR SAINT-JACQUES

I walked from the Gare du Nord to the capital's historical centre. As well as Nerval's books, I had taken care to slip into my bag a guide to modern and ancient Paris written in the 1920s which I had bought from a second-hand dealer in Boston. In the middle of the book was a very colourful map and every time I consulted it I circled in pen the names of the main roads, bridges, squares and monuments which captured my imagination.

Whistling, I headed down Boulevard de Magenta and then Rue du Faubourg-Saint-Denis before turning down Rue Réaumur on to Boulevard de Sébastopol. At the top of Rue de Turbigo, I made my way through narrow streets with delightfully evocative names: Rue aux Ours, Rue Quincampoix, Rue Aubry-le-Boucher, Rue Brisemiche, and so on.

At the bend in Rue Saint-Bon, I reached Tour Saint-Jacques, so dear to Nerval. The monument was all that remained of the old church of Saint-Jacques-de-la-Boucherie whose refurbishment had been paid for by Nicolas Flamel, the famous alchemist.

The tower took pride of place in the middle of a small square filled with trees and flowers. Somewhere in this garden was the spot where the poet had come to hang himself that night in January 1855. Unless it was fifty yards further along where the solemn Théâtre des Nations had since been built[2]. In Nerval's time, the area didn't have the respectable feel it has today. It had been a jumble of dark alleyways and sordid passageways where scoundrels and down-

and-outs loitered. That was before Baron Haussmann's engineers 'civilised' Old Paris for ever.

The day after Nerval's death, Alexandre Dumas, Théophile Gautier, Roger de Beauvoir and, to a lesser extent, Arsène Houssaye expressed serious doubts about the suicide theory. They thought that their friend had been the victim of one of the local ruffians.

I remember talking one evening, in a pub in Aldgate, to a music hall lighting engineer who had worked in Paris a few years earlier at the Théâtre des Nations. According to him, when work had been carried out in the building's basement at the beginning of the 1910s, engineers, comparing the city maps with those of sixty years before, had noticed that the bars of the cellar window where Nerval had been found hanged at the end of a thin rope corresponded exactly to the current position of the prompter's box. What's more, if the usherettes were to be believed, on some evenings the poet's ghost wandered between the rows of stalls after the performance. There was even a story that Sarah Bernhardt's prompter was the ghost in person. However, I suspect that my companion, who was partial to whisky, was trying to pull the wool over my eyes to some extent.

I rested for a few minutes on a bench in Square Saint-Jacques, opposite the tower, and then, as evening began to fall, started looking for a hotel.

Having briefly studied the neighbourhood, I decided on an establishment in Rue de la Verrerie next to the church of Saint-Merri where the writer of the future had been christened, and a stone's throw from the building in Rue Saint-Martin where he'd been born on 22 May 1808.

I went up to my room to drop off my luggage. The walls and ceiling were crisscrossed with beams and the rustic furniture didn't seem to have been replaced since the days of Rue de la Vieille-Lanterne.

It was the perfect place for me. Here I could easily immerse myself in the writer's work, wander where he had wandered at night, try to understand what had been going through his mind and perhaps even establish the exact circumstances of his death.

'I am the other,' he had written in the margin of a book[4].

I wanted to be *him* for a few days.

The next day, Wednesday 17 October, after a disturbed night of fraught and chaotic dreams which I was unable to remember upon waking, and a quick morning stroll on the banks of the Seine, I spent much of the day in my room, reading Nerval's biography. It was long past midday when I eventually decided to go out for lunch at the Café des Innocents. A hundred and fifty years earlier it had been the site of a cemetery of the same name. At the end of the fourteenth century, on a panel there Nicolas Flamel (him again) had had a 'man in black' drawn on one of its pillars, directly facing the alchemic figures supposedly taken from the book of Abraham the Jew.

In Paris, more than anywhere else, history had left its mark on the present. For those who were able to *see*, reality consisted of more than just the fleeting con tours of beings and things. Wherever the eyes of those who could see fell, on the corner of every street, on nearly every wall, between every join in the cobblestones, they could perceive another layer beneath the superficial layer of reality. It looked similar but was very different and slightly out of step, a little like the anaglyphs whose technique Louis Lumière was refining in his workshops in order to screen three-dimensional films. Perhaps one day, simply wearing a pair of stereoscopic glasses in the street would make a new view of life possible – richer, more profound, more real, carved out of the depths of time, where past and present would be visible simultaneously.

After lunch I pushed the remains of my meal away and opened

Aristide Marie's book, which I always had with me. On one of the last pages, an extract from the register of the morgue (then located north-east of Pont Saint-Michel on Rue du Marché-Neuf) was reproduced with the observations made by the state pathologist, Dr Devergie, on 26 January. Also reproduced was the complete text of the death certificate drawn up on 29 January at the town hall in the ninth arrondissement. These were about the only facts available. Thirty pages earlier, in a very obscure sentence, Aristide Marie intimated that documents from the investigation had been destroyed. What had happened? Was there any hope of ever finding them again?

For now, I intended to visit the archives of the new Forensic Institute at Place Mazas near Quai de la Rapée.

As the weather remained fine, I decided to walk along the Seine. Emerging on to Rue de Rivoli, I had just reached Tour Saint-Jacques, in front of Cavelier's statue of Pascal, when I heard someone behind me calling my name.

'Singleton! Singleton! Is that you?'

'Inspector Fourier!' I exclaimed, delighted to see the familiar face of the detective from the Sûreté, who was striding towards me.

'Ah, my friend!' he cried breathlessly, warmly shaking my outstretched hand. 'But it's Superintendent now, you know. I've been promoted!'

'Of course, how could I have forgotten! This summer the *Daily Mail* reported at length on the exploits of Superintendent Fourier. That great figure of the Paris police force who managed to put behind bars the famous Bosco, big-time thief and the kind of colourful, elusive character only to be found in France!'

'Well, well!' he exclaimed, smoothing the long, solitary lock of hair which ran from one side of his head to the other. 'I'm delighted to see that the reputation of our men is starting to cross the Channel. Give it a little time and Scotland Yard will be visiting our offices in

Rue des Saussaies to study our methods. In any case, my dear friend, without you and your faithful partner I don't think we would ever have got the better of the infamous Billancourt studios killer.'

I won't dwell on the case of the Cut-throat with the Broken Watch which I referred to earlier. One of these days I intend to gather together all the documents and notes made at the time and write the whole story down. In the meantime, all the reader needs to know is that in the winter of 1933 James and I made the acquaintance of the kind and scrupulous Edmond Fourier from the Sûreté Générale. Although the investigation had been particularly sensitive (the idea of working with two amateur detectives was nothing less than sacrilege for some members of his organisation), Fourier, who had initiated the collaboration, always demonstrated full confidence in us. In the end, it served him well.

With his customary tweed suit, tweed overcoat, thin moustache, bowler hat and swordstick, Superintendent Fourier was the archetypal French policeman. He was a mixture of Juve, Tirauclair and Chantecoq![5] When I was with him I felt as though the shadow of Fantômas was about to appear on a rooftop or that the agile dandy overtaking us on the pavement was none other than Arsène Lupin returning from another burglary at a prince's residence or the Crédit Lyonnais on Boulevard des Italiens.

Edmond Fourier was about fifty-four or fifty-five and the son of ironmongers from the Franche-Comté region but he had lived in Paris, in Rue Cadet, for a long time. His humble origins had taught him common sense and realism, which often paid off. He had joined the Sûreté Générale at the age of twenty-seven, a few years after Prime Minister Clemenceau had set up his *brigades mobiles*, the famous Tiger Brigades, to counterbalance the all-powerful Préfecture de Police. Fourier was one of the stars of the Sûreté which, since its creation in 1820, had always suffered from comparisons with its rival. The large-scale reorganisation of the State's police force the previous April had also seen the resources and remit of the Sûreté increase considerably so that it now had national powers. The staff of the Sûreté and the Préfecture were not quite ready to bury the hatchet but the new set-up did at least give each institution precise boundaries.[6]

'But I see no sign of that wag Trelawney,' remarked Fourier, pretending to look left and right over his shoulder in case my six-foot-three friend was hiding in the policeman's short shadow.

'James stayed in London but he'll be joining me soon. At the moment, I imagine he's finding it very difficult to resist the siren call of your city.'

'Do I take it then that you are … uh … what one might call "on holiday"?'

All of a sudden his deceptively disinterested tone made me realise that meeting Superintendent Fourier like this wasn't simply a coincidence. Although he undoubtedly had all the qualities required of a detective, his acting skills left much to be desired. I remembered that the evening before, as I had left a brasserie on Rue Saint-Martin near my hotel, and then again that morning during a short stroll among the booksellers on Quai de Montebello, I had noticed a thickset individual with a broken nose like a boxer and short black crew cut hair whom I vaguely recognised but couldn't place at the time. Now, the detective's mischievous expression instantly provided me with the fellow's name: Raymond Dupuytren who worked for Superintendent Fourier at the Sûreté Nationale and whom I'd met on several occasions in January 1933.

The French police had certainly not improved in the field of domestic espionage. When the press wanted to mock it, didn't they refer to it as the *national secret*?

'Come, Superintendent,' I said. 'Don't keep me in suspense any longer. Tell me why you wanted to see me — I know you've been following me. Wouldn't it have been easier just to ask me to come to Rue des Saussaies?'

'Ha ha! I see I still can't get anything past you! As for making you come to the Sûreté, there was no point. I got wind that you'd left the Hôtel Saint-Merri and since I happened to be near Île de la Cité this afternoon, it seemed natural to pay you a little courtesy visit.'

'Only this time you almost missed me. I was about to go to Bercy.'

'You're right, my dear friend! Anyway, enough of this banter! I imagine you're still fond of cases which baffle even the most intelligent of men?'

'Well …'

'I'm investigating a rather strange case that would appeal to you! The death of the Marquis de Brindillac. Have you heard about it?'

'No.'

'How come? Haven't you read the papers?'

'Since I arrived I haven't opened a single one. Strange as it may sound, you see me before you but it's just an illusion. In reality, I'm in 1855. Busy solving an incredible mystery.'

'How frustrating!' said the detective, who knew my liking for long literary excursions. 'I don't know what kind of case you're dealing with but you should know that events every bit as extraordinary are happening in 1934.'

'I don't doubt it.'

'It'll be worth it, I promise. You've never heard anything like it, even in a novel.'

'Don't get carried away!'

'Give me half an hour, Singleton. Just enough time to bring you up to date.'

'You're making my mouth water, Superintendent! Go on then, tell me what's happened.'

III

DEADLY SLEEP

We sat in a café on Rue de Rivoli. Through the window I could see the vast form of the Hôtel de Ville and, in front, the old Place de Grève where so many villains had been quartered in the Middle Ages and much of the nobility had been decapitated during the Revolution.

'Four days ago,' began Fourier, savouring his first sip of an excellent red wine from Burgundy, 'the old Marquis de Brindillac was found dead in his bedroom at his home, Château B——, between Dourdan and Étampes in the Paris region. He was a renowned physiologist, highly thought of by his peers, who spent his life studying the human brain and particularly the mysteries of sleep. A jovial and passionate man, he was also rather eccentric. He had always been interested in analysing and understanding dreams, something which had led him to a fairly unorthodox kind of research over the past few years. As luck would have it, the fellow died in his sleep!

'At quarter past ten in the morning on Saturday 13 October, last Saturday that is, the Marquise de Brindillac, whose bedroom is just opposite her husband's, was worried when he didn't answer after she knocked on his door. Usually, at that time he had been up for a while and was already hard at work. As the doors to the Marquis's bedroom, study and library were all locked from the inside (the three rooms lead into each other through connecting doors), she alerted a servant who, with the help of the gardener, forced open the bedroom door. They found the poor man dead in bed in his nightclothes, the sheets kicked down around his legs. The most incredible thing was the look on his face: it was frozen in an expression of intense fear, a fear very difficult to explain because his eyes were closed, as if the terror had come not from something external, brutally waking him, but, on the contrary, had gripped him from inside sleep itself.

'A doctor was called, followed a few minutes later by a gendarme. For the doctor there was no doubt that the Marquis had died from heart failure, after a violent panic attack which had weakened him. However, he thought it unlikely that one could die of fright and, given the unusual nature of the tragedy (in all his career he had never seen such an expression of terror on anyone's face!), he declared that he couldn't issue a death certificate stating that the Marquis had died of natural causes. Consequently, the gendarme arranged for the body to be removed and the Versailles public prosecutor, who was hurriedly contacted, decided to carry out an autopsy as is required in such a situation.

'The body was transported to the morgue in Étampes. On Monday morning the pathologist delivered his report and he, too, concluded that the Marquis had died of heart failure caused by a night terror. However, he emphasised that the Marquis de Brindillac was in excellent health when he went to bed, if it can be put that way. No heart or respiratory problems, no sign of bleeding to the brain. The report confirmed that the victim had died of fright but nothing more was known about what had frightened him.

'But did that really matter? After three days of fruitless investigation, that was what everyone was beginning to wonder. The Marquis was seventy-two; at that age anyone can be unlucky, even if they're fit and well. A sudden shock and that's it! And anyway, perhaps we were mistaken in thinking we saw terror on his face? Maybe we should just have seen it as a sign of suffering, the torment of a body until then lucky in life and which, suddenly, feels abandoned by it. Good heavens, when you die you rarely look happy about it! Between you and me, that opinion was hardly outrageous and those closest to him went along with it: the Marquis's widow, his colleagues at the Académie des Sciences, who know a thing or two about reports and diagnosis. Why, even his friends at the Meta-whatsit Institute, who have made a speciality out of splitting hairs, didn't call for a more comprehensive investigation.'

'Do you mean the Institut Métapsychique?'

'That's the one. A bunch of cranks, doctors and scientists, often very well known in their fields, who believe in life after death and that man has certain occult powers. Do you know it?'

'I've heard of it. There's a similar society in London.'

'If I am to believe the gendarmes' report, the poor Marquise appears to regret that the most eccentric aspect of her husband's character ended up getting the better of him. She's sure that, in some way, it was these new ideas that killed him. Or, more precisely, the enormous enthusiasm he'd put into his latest research. Although he had retired from his position as a professor at the Faculty of Medicine, he had recently thrown himself into some fairly unconventional work with unbridled energy.'

'What work was this?'

'The Marquis — because, despite his status as a doctor of medicine and a professor of physiology, the good man preferred people to use his noble title! — the Marquis claimed, for example, that one could control one's dreams and move at will through entirely invented dream landscapes.'

'My word!'

'Indeed. Anyway, in the light of the results of the local gendarmes' investigation, on Tuesday the public prosecutor decided to close the case. And that's when one of those blasted journalists waded in, digging up a story which goes back three months.'

Fourier took a copy of *Paris-Soir* out of his coat pocket. The newspaper was dated the day before; it had been folded to highlight one article in particular.

DEADLY SLEEP

Could this be the beginning of a terrifying series of murders? As the justice system, with its usual haste, prepares to close the case concerning the death of the Marquis de Brindillac in his sleep (see yesterday's edition), will the following information be enough to make the magistrates and detectives think again? On the night of 25 August in Montmartre, Paris, the poet Pierre Ducros died in a similar way to the eminent physiologist at the end of last week. At the time, our newspaper reported that, having gone quietly to sleep in his bed the evening before, Pierre Ducros was found dead the following morning by Suzanne Ducros, his sister and only relative, a painter who shared his flat in Rue des Martyrs and had a studio on the floor above. According to Mademoiselle Ducros, her brother had his eyes closed when she entered his room to open the curtains and he looked terrified – lest we need reminding, exactly like our unfortunate Marquis. Pierre Ducros, for a time a member of the Surrealist movement, had come to attention a few months earlier with his magnificent collection of poems entitled La Forme des rêves.

This summer, following a half-hearted – to say the least – investigation by the Préfecture de Police, the Seine public prosecutor closed the case, concluding that the young man had died of heart failure while he slept. After the death of Auguste de Brindillac last Saturday it is disturbing to note just how deadly sleep has become recently in the Paris region. Above all, it is deplorable that, until now, not one of our brilliant sleuths has been bothered by this 'coincidence'. That goes for the gendarmerie in charge of the Brindillac affair, as well as the Préfecture or the Sûreté. The people will be reassured to learn that the steps taken in April by Doumergue's cabinet have already borne fruit: after reorganising the various forces, none is any better than the others. Frenchmen and -women, you may sleep soundly in your beds!

The article was signed J.L.

I couldn't help smiling as I read the journalist's final statement about the incompetence of the legal system. So that was why Fourier wanted to see me. The police's methods were being questioned again and the critics had to be silenced. He thought that my experience in complex cases, full of false leads and superficial elements, meant that I would be able to give him a sensible opinion on this unlikely affair.

'Of course,' he continued, 'the other newspapers have just followed *Paris-Soir*'s lead. *Le Matin*, *Paris-Midi*, *Le Petit Journal*, *L'Excelsior*, *Le Petit Parisien*, they're all saying the same thing. I was summoned to the chief's study earlier. And do you know what? The Versailles public prosecutor has done a complete volte-face. Not only is he not closing the case, he's opening a preliminary judicial investigation.'

'Why, for goodness' sake?'

'Fear of scandal, of course! It mustn't be said that the justice system has yet again failed to seek out the truth!⁷ And what's more, the Justice Minister has decided that the investigation will be carried out by the Sûreté Nationale. It's now up to me, in collaboration with the examining magistrate, to shed light on the death of the Marquis de Brindillac. If he did die of fright, we have to find out what

32

frightened him. The Préfecture has been asked to discreetly reopen the Ducros file. The news hasn't been made public so as not to give the impression the writer of the article was right but the press will find out soon enough. Ah! It's a nice snub to the Préfet de Police!'

'Why isn't the Préfecture dealing with the Brindillac case?' I asked, handing back the newspaper.

'It's a question of divisional authority. The Préfecture only covers Paris and the Seine *département*. As the Marquis died in his château in Seine-et-Oise, it's the Sûreté's responsibility.'

'And have you been able to find out any more about the poet's death?'

'I've just left Préfecture headquarters. I had to move heaven and earth to get access to the report but good heavens! I wasn't going to leave before they showed it to me. In fact the case is similar to the Marquis's in all respects. Young Ducros died in his sleep, suddenly, as though gripped by extreme fear. The sheets were tangled as if he had tried to fight or free himself from some powerful pressure. But, according to the doctor who came to certify the death, there were no injuries, marks or obvious lesions on his body. His sister, who slept in the next room, had heard him groan in his sleep. She had got up and noticed that he was dreaming. His health was delicate. Those close to him described him as depressive, nervous, tormented, and of a weak constitution. His heart may have given out as a result of an extraordinary kind of hallucination. In those circumstances, his death, however distressing, was not entirely incomprehensible. To put it crudely, he had been living on borrowed time!'

'Was there an autopsy?'

'Yes but there again, the results aren't particularly revealing. The toxicology examination didn't indicate the presence of any narcotic substances. It's a pity – that would have solved the problem.'

'It's certainly very strange.'

'In both cases, one thing is certain: the victims died of sudden heart failure related to an unusually intense fear. The doctors called to the scene thought as much and the pathologists confirmed it. So, if they died of fright, well, for heaven's sake, there must be a reason!'

'Is it possible to die from a nightmare?' I wondered aloud, trying to imagine the face of someone stricken by terror in his sleep.

'I'm not sure about that, but I am sure that the Brindillac case can no longer be considered in isolation. Now the problem must be examined from every angle. It won't take much for the Sûreté to be accused of botching the job too.'

'From every angle? So you're not excluding criminal activity?'

'Now don't get carried away, Singleton! Tell me how a murderer could have entered the Marquis's bedroom. Let me remind you that the doors to his rooms were locked from the inside and the windows too. And as for Ducros, his sister was sleeping next door. If anyone had broken in, she would have realised.'

'Like me, you read detective novels, Superintendent. The crime is often committed in a locked room: no one can enter, no one can leave and yet someone has been killed.'

'That is certainly commonplace in England but it is less common here, I can assure you. What's more, my friend, in your novels things are clear-cut. The victim is found poisoned, stabbed or shot. There are three drops of blood indicating that a crime has been committed. But there's nothing like that here. In the pathologists' reports no mention is made of any violence against the scientist or the man of letters.'

'Was Ducros's flat locked?'

'Double locked.'

The superintendent drummed his fingers on the newspaper. 'This reporter has managed to create havoc! As if we didn't have enough problems already with the controversy over the death of Minister

Barthou[8]. Not to mention the repercussions of the Stavisky case. The public have a terrible impression of both politicians and the police. One spark is all it would take for the whole thing to blow up.'

A sentence in the newspaper caught my eye. I hadn't taken in all of the relevant information the first time I read it.

> *Pierre Ducros, for a time a member of the Surrealist movement, had come to attention a few months earlier with his magnificent collection of poems entitled* La Forme des rêves.

'Hmm!' I said, holding a match up to the end of my cigarette holder.

For a few moments I was distracted by the cloud of blue smoke wafting around my head, drifting slowly towards the large electric light on the ceiling.

I had read numerous texts by the Surrealists, particularly those by André Breton (*Nadja* and the two manifestos). I knew that they were fascinated by dreams; indeed dreams were one of their main sources of inspiration. The title of Pierre Ducros's recent collection clearly indicated that his interest in the study of dreams hadn't faded either. As for the Marquis de Brindillac, as Fourier had said, he was a scientist who had devoted himself to the analysis of sleep phenomena and whose career had been taking a psychic turn for some time. Both men believed that their dreams were of major importance. Now, they had both died within a few months of each other in extraordinary circumstances, from a violent, incomprehensible fear while their minds wandered through the land of dreams … or nightmares.

Was it just a coincidence? Or was the *Paris-Soir* journalist was right? Was there a mystery surrounding the deaths of Brindillac and Ducros? Or had the journalist just come up with the Deadly Sleep phrase because it made a catchy headline?

'How do you intend to proceed, Superintendent?' I asked, realising that I was more intrigued by this story than I had expected.

'Firstly, by paying a visit to Château B——. I have an appointment with the examining magistrate appointed by the Versailles public prosecutor early tomorrow afternoon. Just between you and me, until yesterday the Justice Minister wanted nothing to do with the death of the Marquis de Brindillac, the public prosecutor couldn't care less either and the general public likewise. Now, everyone wants to stick their oar in.'

With a gulp Fourier swallowed the rest of his Burgundy. Wiping a drop of wine from his moustache, he declared in a detached tone: 'I say! I've just had a thought. Since you're on holiday in our beautiful city, why don't you come to the château with me tomorrow? You can share your thoughts with me. You can make room in your schedule, surely, to give up a day to shed some light on this case.'

I couldn't help smiling. The trap was a little obvious but it had worked perfectly. As Fourier had said, it was certainly mysterious and I also found it rather gratifying, that at the age of twenty-five, my services were required by one of Paris's leading detectives. Besides, I'd promised James that I wouldn't let a case slip through my fingers if it presented itself and that I'd alert him as soon as possible. And, in return, Fourier could help me gain access to certain archives for my investigation into Nerval's death.

'Yes, yes,' I said. 'But I warn you, tomorrow evening I will return to 1855.'

'Glad to hear it!' retorted Fourier. 'Let's meet tomorrow at half past eleven at the Gare d'Orsay.'

'What? Aren't we going by car?'

'Our vehicle has been at the garage for the last two weeks. The Sûreté Nationale might have been allocated more funds but it's hard to tell sometimes.'

We had spent longer than expected chatting in the café. Outside, night had almost fallen.

'I must go!' exclaimed Fourier, looking at his watch. 'As we speak, the head of the Sûreté and the Préfet de Police are meeting the Interior Minister, Monsieur Sarraut. I imagine he is going to demand close collaboration between our two forces.'

He threw some coins down on the table. As he shook my hand, he suddenly looked at me curiously.

'By the way, what is this investigation which means I have the pleasure of your company here?'

'The death of Gérard de Nerval.'

'What? The poet?'

'The very same.'

'But wasn't it suicide?'

'That's exactly what I'd like to know for certain!'

From the brasserie, I headed towards the Seine. My expedition to Quai de la Rapée was no longer relevant. Crossing Pont-au-Change, I leant over the stone parapet for a moment and contemplated a passing *bateau-mouche* with its blinding headlights, which was carrying a handful of tourists awed by the splendours of Paris. The season was over but the fine weather had prolonged the euphoric feeling of summer. Something told me that things were going to take a turn for the worse though. Was it the night itself, which was getting darker by the minute on the horizon, far from the lights of the Seine? Was it the icy shiver that ran down my spine despite the relatively balmy air? Was it the silty black water swirling in the middle of the river and which continued churning long after the boat had passed as if some obscure, ancient underground force was extending its empire to the world's surface?

I continued on my way via Boulevard Saint-Germain and Quai Saint-Bernard up to the Jardin des Plantes. As I passed a post office, I stopped to send James a telegram.

STAYING AT HÔTEL SAINT-MERRI, NEAR TOUR
SAINT-JACQUES, ROOM 14.
SUPERINTENDENT FOURIER REQUESTS ASSISTANCE IN BRINDILLAC
CASE (SEE *PARIS-SOIR* OF 16 OCTOBER ON
MYSTERY OF 'DEADLY SLEEP').
STRANGE FEELING.
ANDREW

After dining at a restaurant in Bastille, I returned to my hotel where I spent the rest of the evening reading.

On the two days prior to his death, Gérard de Nerval had visited his friends, one after the other. He was penniless. Several days beforehand he had left his room at the Normandie and found himself homeless. Temperatures outside had dropped to freezing. Those who received him in their homes for a few minutes and others who met him in a reading room or a bar at Les Halles were worried when they saw him leave with nowhere to go, heading out into the snow and the cold, but they knew that there was no way of stopping him. He turned up at the home of Paul Lacroix, a scholar who used the pen name Bibliophile Jacob. He went to Joseph Méry's but his friend was away. At a reception given by Madame Person, an actress, he had appeared gay and cheerful.

On the fateful evening of 25 January, on the banks of the Seine near the Hôtel de Ville, Nerval told his friend, the painter Chenavard, who had made it his duty to accompany him in his wandering, that 'the way forward is clear; it must be followed. The baton is in the hand of the traveller.'

Then he had walked alone for a long time, taking any street he came to before, at the end of that evening, heading for Place du Châtelet – and Rue de la Vieille-Lanterne …

* * *

Late that night, I sat up in bed, my eyes feverish, disoriented by a dream so vivid that for a moment I believed that the scene had really just taken place in front of me. As soon as I had gathered my wits about me and, responding instinctively to the order I had been given in the dream, I grabbed the sheet of paper and pencil at the end of the bed and quickly noted down everything I had seen.

DREAM I
NIGHT OF 17–18 OCTOBER

Bedtime: 10.30 p.m.
Approximate time when fell asleep: 12.15 a.m.
Time awoken: 3.05 a.m.

I am stretched out on my bed and dreaming that I am asleep.

I am asleep and yet I am perfectly aware that I am in my room at the Hôtel Saint-Merri. In the semi-darkness I can make out the whitewashed walls, the beams crisscrossing the ceiling, the books on the table, my clothes on the back of the chair. I can feel the clean, starched sheets against my skin. A faint odour of wood and furniture polish wafts through the air.

I dream, aware that I am dreaming. I can actually see myself sleeping. It is a strange sensation – gentle and euphoric.

Suddenly, although I remember closing the door and locking it, I hear the handle turn, the hinges creak, and the door slowly opens. The figure of a woman is visible in the feeble light from the corridor. I cannot yet make out her face but I recognise her immediately: it is the stranger from the steamer. She is dressed in a green silk tunic, her feet are bare and her blond hair floats over her shoulders as if held up by invisible fingers. Her

39

presence casts a milky light on the objects around her.

As she moves into the room, my heart begins to beat so hard it almost jumps out of my chest. I would like her to come up to me, to sit down and take my hand. Instead, she heads towards the window, picks up a sheet of paper and a pencil lying on the table and slowly returns to the bed and lays them on the floor.

She stares at me without blinking. She is even more beautiful than I remembered. I feel she is about to leave me; I want to talk to her, implore her to stay a few more minutes but I have barely opened my mouth before she puts her fingers to my lips and commands my silence. Her skin is soft, surprisingly soft.

Then she steps away from me, still without uttering a word. As she moves towards the corridor, she repeatedly points to the objects on the floor. The sheet of paper and the pencil.

Before disappearing, she smiles at me as if to console me, encouraging me to be patient, telling me that she will come back. I follow her with my eyes until she's gone. Then the noise of the door closing wakes me up.

NOTES UPON WAKING

1. As I recall, the sheet of paper and the pencil were on the table last night. But memories can be deceptive; this one must be deceptive. Without realising it, I put them at the end of the bed before going to sleep.

2. The sexual charge of the dream is undeniable and is not unknown in the malaise afflicting me. But why did the young woman insist that I record the contents of the dream on paper?

3. (Note added at 8.15 a.m.) Took a long time to fall asleep again. When I got up, I checked that the bedroom door was locked. It was.

In the morning, I bought a notebook at a shop on Rue Saint-Honoré and then sat outside a café where I wrote up the dream properly, having scribbled it down at three o'clock in the morning almost automatically, together with the observations I had forced myself to record with as much clarity as I could at the time.

This I christened my dream notebook. It would come to play an important role throughout my life.

Clearly, dreams were to be significant during my time in Paris. Having come to find out the real cause of the death of Gérard de Nerval, for whom dreams and reality had constantly merged recklessly, I myself was now experiencing the ambiguous nature of the realm of dreams, at once so alluring and so pernicious.

Just for a moment, feeling suddenly fearful, I almost turned back and took the first train to London. But, as I was leaving the café, somewhere a bell chimed eleven o'clock and I instinctively hurried in the direction of the Seine, cut through the Tuileries Gardens and, crossing Pont du Carrousel, reached the Gare d'Orsay where Fourier and his constable, Dupuytren, were waiting for me on the platform for the express train to Orléans.

IV

AT CHÂTEAU B—

When we came out of Étampes station, the driver of an old-fashioned four-cylinder Colda called over to us.

'Superintendent Fourier?'

'That's me!'

'I am Monsieur Breteuil's chauffeur – he's the examining magistrate. He sent me. He's waiting for you at the château.'

'How considerate!'

We drove for about three miles before reaching the entrance to the estate. Two sergeants were on duty, keeping an eye on the reporters and the curious who were crowding around the gates. Ever since the publication of the much-read article in *Paris-Soir* all comings and goings had been carefully checked in order to try to gather any snippets of information.

The gates were opened to let us through and the car sped up the drive leading to the château.

It was a charming manor house, a relic from a rich past – one of those houses that make the Île-de-France region so appealing today. The façade was fairly wide and two storeys high. Behind the imposing main body of the building were the narrow roofs of two medieval towers which could be seen from the direction of the village.

In fact, the château hadn't been built in the Middle Ages, but at the end of the sixteenth century and altered several times during the eighteenth and nineteenth centuries. One restoration project had left more of a mark than the others – there were signs that the front of the building had been added to an older section at the back or had at least been rebuilt from top to bottom along more modern lines.

As Superintendent Fourier had had time to explain to me on the journey, the Marquis de Brindillac had bought Château B— twenty years earlier to escape the hustle and bustle of the capital which had become unsuitable for the work he was carrying out.

Auguste Jean Raoul de Brindillac had been born on 28 April 1862. His father, Ernest Léon Honoré, had been an army surgeon, who in 1859 had married Marquise Joséphine Amélie de la Batte, granddaughter of a general during the Empire. They had had three children: Honoré, Auguste and Joséphine. After the death of his first wife, Auguste de Brindillac had in 1899 married Sophie Mathilde Van Doorsen, heiress of a wealthy Dutch family originally from Haarlem, with whom he had had two children: René, who had died in a hunting accident in 1926, and Amélie.

The Marquis de Brindillac, like his father before him, developed a vocation for surgery and anatomy very early on. He qualified as a doctor at the École de Médecine de Paris. An admirer of Bouillaud, and particularly Broca, he was passionate about physiology and the study of the human brain. He spent time at the laboratories of Marey, Berthelot and Vulpian. Following in the footsteps of Paul Broca, he focused his early scientific research on a better understanding of the limbic system or rhinencephalon, and on identifying the centre of speech in the brain. In 1894 he wrote a *Clinical and Physiological Treatise on the Location of the Language Centre in the Brain* which is still a standard work on the subject and led to him being elected to the Académie de Médecine de Paris in 1896. He was a professor of clinical medicine and physiology at the Hôpital de la Charité for a long time. The publication of his *Clinical Treatise on Disorders of the Nervous System* in 1909 definitively established his reputation as a leading scientist. In 1911 he was appointed dean of the Faculty of Medicine in Paris. In November 1924, he was elected to the

Académie des Sciences. The Marquis was without doubt one of the country's greatest minds.

The chauffeur parked on the drive, near the main entrance to the château, next to two saloon cars in the deep-blue colour of the French gendarmerie.

As we climbed the front steps, a short man of about sixty, whose hair and small goatee were as white as his skin, came to greet us. He was accompanied by a man who looked almost identical – same build, same pointed beard – but with slightly blonder hair, and twenty years younger. Behind him, a bald, plump individual was talking to a gendarme in the entrance hall.

'Superintendent Fourier I presume?' said the pale man. 'I'm Judge Breteuil and I've been appointed by the Versailles prosecutor's study to handle this sad affair. Let me introduce Monsieur Bezaine, my clerk. Oh, and this is Monsieur d'Arnouville, the prosecutor's deputy, who was just leaving, and Second Lieutenant Rouzé, from the local gendarmerie.'

He indicated the two men from the hall who, having seen us, had come out on to the steps to join us.

'Monsieur, let me thank you for sending a car to the station,' said the superintendent to the examining magistrate.

'Monsieur Breteuil considered, quite rightly, that it was essential for you to reach the château as quickly as possible,' the prosecutor's deputy interjected with feigned politeness.

'It would certainly have been a pity if we'd lost our way.'

'I was given to understand this morning that the police were about to open a new investigation into the death of this Pierre Ducros,' continued the deputy. 'The press is so powerful nowadays it can influence the decisions of the Seine public prosecutor's study and the Préfecture!'

'I was under the impression that the Versailles prosecutor's sudden volte-face was similarly influenced by the publication of a certain article.'

'If you're alluding to the decision to open a judicial inquiry into the affair which brings us here, you're wrong. The public prosecutor never intended to close the case and he does not allow himself to be dictated to by anyone, especially not journalists.'

'That is all to his credit.'

'One thing is certain – the police don't need another scandal.'

'Neither does the justice system.'

'Oh! But we haven't reached that point yet, gentlemen!' the examining magistrate intervened, fearing that tensions were rising. 'Before you arrived, Superintendent, we – the prosecutor's deputy, Second Lieutenant Rouzé and myself – were discussing the article published in *Paris-Soir*. At the moment, the press is doing everything it can to create a scandal. By the way, do we know who this J.L. is?'

'His name is Jacques Lacroix. No one has seen him at the newspaper's offices in Rue du Louvre or at his home since Tuesday. It's a pity. I have a great deal to say to him. We'll soon track him down though.'

'Would it be indiscreet to ask your opinion of the two deaths, Superintendent Fourier?' asked the prosecutor's deputy.

'Well, I'm only here to investigate the death of the poor Marquis! And my investigations are only just beginning. It would surely be more instructive to hear Monsieur Rouzé's point of view since he's been involved in the Brindillac case all along?'

The gendarme opened his mouth to speak but Fourier had not finished and turned to me.

'By the way, allow me to introduce Monsieur Andrew Fowler Singleton. Monsieur Singleton and his associate, Monsieur Trelawney, who is currently detained in London, helped the French police with a case that was in the news last year.'

'Singleton! Trelawney! Yes, of course, I remember it well!' exclaimed the examining magistrate. 'Your names certainly made the papers at the time. I didn't realise you were so young though.'

After his initial enthusiasm, the magistrate's face darkened, as he reflected that, all things considered, my presence would cause a few problems.

'Good heavens, Superintendent,' he remarked with some embarrassment towards me, 'do you not think that this investigation has had enough publicity already?'

'On the contrary,' retorted Fourier, unflustered. 'As the prosecutor's deputy confirmed, we need all the help we can get to solve this case as soon as possible. What's more, if, as the Versailles prosecutor's study believed less than twenty-four hours ago, the only strange thing about this death is the rather unusual circumstances surrounding it, then everything will be sorted out in no time. The Sûreté is going to use its expertise. With the help of our friend here, I wager that the mystery will melt away within two days. If the Préfecture acts with the same efficiency, it will be all to the good.'

'That is exactly the attitude Monsieur d'Armagnac, the Versailles public prosecutor, asked me to convey, "Everything must be resolved as soon as possible!" I am glad that, on this point, we are all in agreement.'

Standing on the top step, the prosecutor's deputy concluded: 'I've just hand-delivered the burial certificate to the Marquise. The funeral can be held this weekend. The Marquise would like the body to be returned to her today but I managed to convince her that, after five days, it was not a good idea. A van from the morgue will therefore take the body to the burial site once the date of the funeral and its location have been fixed. I'm sure that will be a great relief to the family. And now I must leave you, gentlemen. I'm expected in court.'

Monsieur d'Arnouville marched down the steps towards his car and Judge Breteuil invited us to follow him into the château.

'I really don't like the way this investigation is looking,' he said. 'You'll see, it will be one of those cases we never manage to get to the bottom of. And I don't like this atmosphere of suspicion everywhere either. *And* I've been landed with it just a few weeks before I retire.'

'Well, we're here to find the explanation, whatever it is.'

'Dying in your sleep is allowed,' continued the judge. 'It was even considered to be a very good end until last Saturday.'

'It has long been said that Charles Dickens passed away in his sleep,' I said as we entered the building. 'Actually, the celebrated author died of a cerebral haemorrhage.'

Monsieur Breteuil and the clerk, Bezaine, exchanged baffled looks. Clearly, they had no idea what the British writer had to do with Château B——.

'But as for the Marquis de Brindillac,' I continued, 'don't forget the look of terror on his face. Although it's not unheard of to die in one's sleep, it is a little more unusual to die during a nightmare!'

'True, very true,' conceded the judge, rubbing his head.

We had crossed a large hall and stopped in front of a door where a servant was waiting unobtrusively.

'The Marquise and her daughter are in the sitting room,' explained the magistrate. 'They, and the château's staff, were interviewed by Monsieur Rouzé and his men during the first days of the investigation. As Monsieur d'Arnouville said, the burial certificate has just been delivered to them. The ladies are very distressed, gentlemen. Let us proceed with tact and sensitivity.'

We had come to a large stone staircase.

'Of course,' Fourier said. Pointing upstairs, he suggested, 'Why don't we leave them in peace for the moment and ask Monsieur Rouzé to show us where the Marquis was found? That will shed some valuable light on the matter.'

The magistrate agreed with this suggestion. He asked the servant to inform the mistress of the house that he and Superintendent Fourier would speak to her in a few minutes' time and then invited us to follow him.

While the others began to climb the stairs, I stopped in front of a full-length mirror in the hall and considered my reflection. Despite all my efforts to make myself look older, my face remained as youthful as ever. It was exasperating. My bow tie and ragged moustache did nothing to improve the situation. Disappointed, I pushed my trilby more firmly on to my slicked-back hair and, frowning to make myself look sterner, caught up with the group in a few strides.

Upstairs, a corridor ran the full width of the château, dividing it into two parts of roughly equal size. On one side, at the front of the house, were the Marquise de Brindillac's bedroom and her daughter's apartments; on the other, Auguste de Brindillac's rooms, consisting of the bedroom where he had been found dead, a study and a large library. This perfectly geometric distribution was complemented by two spare bedrooms and, at the back, the two circular rooms situated in the towers. The first adjoined the Marquis's library and he used it for his experiments. The second opened on to one of the spare bedrooms but, for reasons still unknown to me, it had been sealed.

To help the reader visualise the layout of the château, I have appended a sketch of the first floor of Château B—, as well as a sketch of Auguste de Brindillac's bedroom (see page 50).

Second Lieutenant Rouzé preceded us to the door of the Marquis's bedroom. When the door had been forced, the servant and gardener had broken the lock so now all it needed was a push. The gendarme did this extremely slowly, as if he feared that the old scientist's body was still lying on the bed.

The room was large. To take it all in, we had to advance a few paces into it in order to see past the area on the right-hand side of

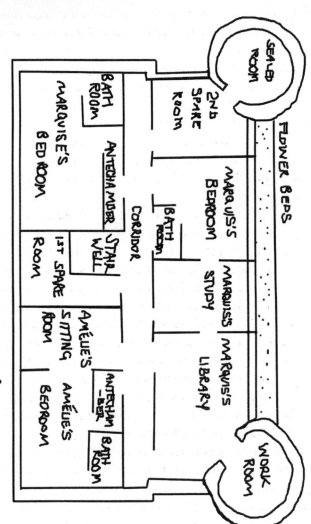

Diagram of the first floor of Château B—

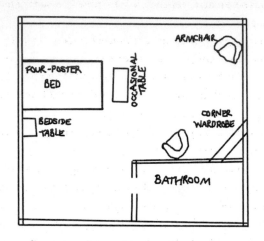

Diagram of the Marquis de Brindillac's bedroom

the entrance which had been turned into a bathroom with all mod cons. Pushed up against the wall, an enormous four-poster bed immediately caught the eye. Its posts, made of high-quality wood, supported large sheets of fabric on which pink, round-faced cherubs flew through bucolic landscapes. From looking at the bed, neatly made under the joyously festooned canopy, the sheets and covers pulled taut without a crease, no one could have imagined the tragedy that had occurred there.

There were a few pieces of furniture in the bedroom (a corner wardrobe, an occasional table, a bedside table and two armchairs) but, apart from a faded wall hanging and a collection of small portraits (mainly of scientists) hung near the door to the study, the room was simply decorated. Stained-glass windows cast an unusual light, creating a subdued atmosphere conducive to reflection at any time of day.

'So, it was here that it happened, was it?' asked the superintendent, approaching the bed.

'Yes,' replied Second Lieutenant Rouzé hoarsely. 'Last Saturday the servant from the château informed the gendarmerie that the Marquis had been found dead in his bed. I got here shortly afterwards, at ten thirty-five. Dr Leduc had arrived before me and was in the process of examining the body.'

'Did anything strike you as strange when you entered the room?' asked the examining magistrate.

'The dead man's face, sir, his face! His expression was one of indescribable terror. Never could I have imagined that such an emotion was possible at the moment of death.'

'And yet,' resumed the judge, slight disappointment in his voice, 'your investigation hasn't been able to determine the cause of this violent emotion.'

'That is true, sir. There was nothing to go on. I fear that it will be the same today ...'

'We'll see, we'll see,' cut in Fourier. 'Did the Marquise, or anyone else in the house, notice anything out of place? Or that anything had disappeared?'

'No, nothing had been touched.'

The superintendent opened one of the two windows to let more light into the room and poked his head outside to assess the height. I joined him, to see for myself.

'I think the theory of criminal activity is looking increasingly unlikely,' he muttered, tugging at his moustache.

It was at least fifteen feet from the bedroom window to the ground. It was impossible to get down the wall using only one's bare hands, particularly as there was a bed of flowering shrubs just beneath the window, which ran right along the façade of the château, and anyone landing there would have left clear traces.

Obviously, there remained the possibility of a ladder. But given that, on the morning of the Marquis's death, the windows had been found locked, just like the doors, then either scenario would imply that one of the three people who had entered the room together (the Marquise, the servant and the gardener) was an accomplice who had closed the window without the other two knowing. Admittedly, this seemed far-fetched.

'Well, as you said, Superintendent, we must look at the problem from all angles.'

While Judge Breteuil questioned Second Lieutenant Rouzé and the clerk, Bezaine, recorded the information in his little notebook, I moved over to the four-poster bed and lightly tapped the wall with my hand. In detective novels the policeman always does that when confronted with a case of murder in a locked room. A secret passageway hidden behind a piece of furniture or a bookcase, a door concealed in a thick wall, and all of a sudden an impenetrable mystery finally begins to unravel.

'Are you looking for something, Monsieur Singleton?' enquired the examining magistrate with an almost comical air of bemusement.

'I'm checking that the walls aren't hollow in places and that there are no doors, niches, cavities or secret alcoves. You'd be surprised at the ingenious hiding places in these old houses.'

The operation didn't yield any results and after a few minutes I dropped to my knees and meticulously examined the floorboards.

'Absolutely nothing!' I said in frustration, getting up. 'This room leads to two others, doesn't it?'

'Yes, the study and the library,' replied the gendarme.

'Were the doors opening on to the corridor locked in these three rooms?'

'Yes, they were.'

'And this one,' I continued, pointing to the door in front of me, between the corner wardrobe and one of the armchairs. 'Was it closed like it is today?'

'Yes, but not locked. Actually, there is no lock or bolt.'

'And what about the door to the library?'

'That one doesn't have a lock either.'

'So these three rooms are a single space in which one can move about freely.'

'That's right.'

'Singleton,' said Fourier, seeing where my thoughts were leading, 'don't you waste your time. Dupuytren, go and search the study and the library. See if there's anything unusual about the floor or walls.'

The faithful Sûreté constable, who until then had been discreetly standing by, calmly carried out the order.

'Why don't we have a look at the other rooms?' continued Fourier.

'An excellent idea,' said the judge, inviting us to go first with a gesture of his hand.

The so-called study, where Dupuytren had rolled up a large threadbare rug and pushed it against the wall in order to begin examining the floor, was a kind of antechamber between the bedroom and the library. It was filled with heavily laden bookshelves (in fact, the entire room was collapsing under the weight of words) and its only furniture was a desk buried under a heap of papers, notes, notebooks and magazines, and a worn armchair.

A few steps away, a second door opened on to the library, the most imposing room of the three and also the most suffocating. Bookshelves took up every inch of space; they covered entire walls and surrounded the windows and door frames. It was as if the idea of having shelves right up to the ceiling had tickled the old Marquis. Against this backdrop of paper, leather and ink, a large mirror hung over the fireplace. Nearby, a wing chair, a desk and, in the middle, an immense table, also covered in paper, were the only pieces of furniture.

On the other side of the library, a large old door, rounded at the top, had been left open. Through the doorway we could see into the work room in the middle of one of the château's towers. Was it the thickness of the heavy door which had managed to hold back the frenzied march of books? In any case, the room didn't seem to suffer from the same excess. 'Only' four or five hundred books occupied the shelves between two narrow windows. Otherwise, the room was remarkably austere, mellow and peaceful, particularly as a bed (yes, a bed, a little camp bed with a pillow and thick blanket) had pride of place in the middle, like an invitation to sleep and dream.

'My word!' exclaimed the superintendent. 'Never in my life have I seen so many books!'

'The Marquis was amazingly methodical in the way he organised them,' I observed, examining the shelves. 'In the study he kept his books on poetry and literature; in the library those on science. Over here we have medicine; over there anatomy; on the other side physiology and so on.'

'And over there?' asked the judge, pointing to the work room.

I went through the low door and approached curiously.

'Spiritualism, paranormal studies, occultism, alchemy — ' I chanted as I consulted their spines.

Behind me I heard the deep voice of Dupuytren.

'Superintendent! There's nothing in the study!'

The idea of carrying out the same task in the library couldn't have excited him but the impassive hound appeared to consider it a point of honour never to reveal his emotions.

'Nothing on the floor and nothing on the walls!' he added.

'I don't really think there's any point exhausting ourselves,' I said, coming out of the tower room. 'We won't find anything in here.'

'Fine, that's enough, Raymond.'

'But there is one thing that's bothering me.'

'What's that?'

'Are you sure that the Marquis's bedroom was exactly as it is now?' I asked Second Lieutenant Rouzé. 'Wasn't there something that was here on Saturday morning which isn't here today?'

'No, sir. As I told the superintendent earlier, nothing has been moved, I'm sure of it. Nothing added, nothing taken away.'

'It's strange. The Marquis was surrounded by books. He was an avid reader to put it mildly.'

'And?' asked Judge Breteuil in surprise.

'Well, someone like that doesn't go to sleep without reading first. It would have been as essential as eating or drinking. It's inconceivable that he went to bed without a book at his side.'

'There was nothing, I can assure you.'

'With all the hours he devoted to reading, I imagine he wanted to do something else when he went to bed,' said Fourier with a shrug.

'I can't believe it,' I said, scratching my nose. 'Either the book was put back accidentally by someone who thought they were being helpful and, with a bit of luck, that person will remember when we ask them. Or ... it's still there!'

I crossed the library and the study briskly and bent down in front of the big four-poster bed. Fourier and Dupuytren followed me, but the examining magistrate, the clerk and the second lieutenant hung back, looking very sceptical.

First, I opened the drawer in the bedside table; it was empty. Then I got down on my hands and knees to look under the bed. The wooden frame was quite low and the bed so wide that I couldn't see anything beyond a few inches.

'Gentlemen!' I called, getting up. 'I need your help to move this bed. Ready? Heave ho!'

We pulled the bed towards the centre of the room. In the middle of a mound of dust was an octavo volume.

'It must have fallen on the floor. Then someone rushing over to the Marquis's body must have accidentally kicked it under the bed.'

I picked it up and wiped the brown leather cover with my hand.

'*Le Comte de Gabalis*,' I read out loud, opening the book. '*Discourses on the Secret Sciences*, by Montfaucon de Villars. Published by Éditions La Connaissance, Paris, 1921.'

I was bursting with excitement. The examining magistrate raised his eyes to heaven.

V

AN UNEXPECTED ENTRANCE

'Madame,' said the examining magistrate, 'I know that Second Lieutenant Rouzé has already spoken to you at length over the last few days but we'd like to ask you some more questions.'

'We're grateful to the justice system for taking my husband's death so seriously. However, I'm sure you'll understand that the disruption has gone on long enough for me and my daughter. The sooner it is over, the better.'

Apart from Dupuytren, who was standing by the window with his arms folded, we were sitting in comfortable armchairs around a low table in the sitting room. A young servant was serving coffee and lemon tea in white china cups.

Opposite me sat the Marquise, a fine-looking woman of about sixty with touches of grey in her hair. She was wearing a long black dress which came down to her ankles. She spoke with a very slight Dutch accent.

On her left was her charming thirty-year-old daughter, Amélie. Her chestnut hair, artistically pulled back and arranged, set off her extraordinarily lively hazel eyes. She was wearing black flannel trousers and a velvet jacket which gave her a tomboyish air.

'Madame,' Judge Breteuil went on, 'you must be aware that the investigation has been reopened because of a possible link between your husband's death and the death of a poet in strangely similar circumstances in Paris this summer.'

'How could I fail to be aware of it? Reporters have been stationed outside the gates of the château since yesterday morning, asking to speak to us. Please assure us that it will soon be over.'

'It is just a matter of a few hours, Madame.'

'Have you read the article that mentions the death of the young man?' asked Superintendent Fourier.

'Yes. Well, my daughter read it to me.'

'Had you already heard of Pierre Ducros?'

'Never.'

'And what do you think of the circumstances in which these two deaths occurred?'

'I don't know, Superintendent,' said the Marquise wearily. 'My husband had got certain unhealthy ideas into his head and it is never good when the imagination takes over from the intellect.'

As she spoke she glanced tearfully at a portrait hanging over the fireplace. It was a fine picture of a man in the prime of life, who had an enormous, badly trimmed beard and a bald pate with a few locks of grey, slighty frizzy hair visible at the temples and the back of his head. He was looking to one side, stiff in evening dress, his chest covered in decorations of all kinds. Nonetheless, his small laughing eyes and restrained smile betrayed a lively, mischievous temperament. Despite the formal pose for the occasion, he looked as if all he wanted to do was throw his tails on the floor and start dancing.

'That portrait of my husband was done when he was elected to the Académie des Sciences in 1924. The artist has captured the different aspects of his personality perfectly. He was sensitive, passionate, a devotee of opera and music. He adored literature and baroque poetry above all else.'

'I've been told that he was particularly curious about the mysteries of nature,' I said, 'and especially the most extraordinary of all: sleep.'

'He'd kept a diary of his dreams since he was fifteen. He liked to boast that few people wrote them down as religiously as he did, and he rarely forgot them. In the morning my children and I were often given a detailed account of a dream which had particularly struck him and he would recount it candidly and unselfconsciously. I think he became a physiologist because of the dreams. He tried, at least at first, to find a scientific explanation for how they are created in the human psyche.'

'When you say, with regard to your husband, that imagination had taken hold of reason,' I continued, 'you are no doubt referring to his psychic work?'

'Yes.'

'When did that begin?'

'Shortly after he was elected to the Académie des Sciences. He met a Professor Charles Richet who made a strong impression on him and who became his friend. Professor Richet is an internationally renowned physiologist. He also founded the Institut Métapsychique[9]. Certain great men who make key discoveries in science and medicine also seem to be taken in by the most hackneyed fantasies.'

'Mother!' Amélie exclaimed. 'I don't believe that Professor Richet led anyone down the wrong path, as you are implying. Papa didn't need anyone else's encouragement to throw himself into the work you disapproved of so much.'

'Yes, my dear, you're probably right. It's grief which makes me speak with such bitterness.'

'I've heard that he was working on the possibility of controlling his dreams. Is that true?'

I had addressed the Marquise. The subject seemed to sadden her greatly and her eyes brimmed with tears again. Amélie, who seemed more at ease in this area, answered for her.

'To some extent, yes. He was convinced that dreams enable one to attain a higher level of knowledge. But he didn't generally discuss the results of his research with us.'

'Did he see people from the Institut Métapsychique often?'

'To begin with, my father visited the Institut at 89 Avenue Niel in Paris once a week. Later, his work became very demanding so he went there less frequently and the metapsychists came to him.'

'Have any of them been here recently?'

'Professor Richet came to see him three weeks before his death; Dr Osty just before that.'[10]

'Over the last few days, did the Marquis receive any visitors, anyone at all?' asked Superintendent Fourier.

'Apart from local people, not that I know of. Only that so-called professor who absolutely insisted on seeing him.'

'Do you know his name?'

'No. At least, I can't remember it. He was a foreigner with a German ... or Austrian ... or maybe Swiss accent.'

'Was he a doctor or a physiologist too?'

'I'm sorry. I can't help you there either.'

'Hmm! I imagine the Marquis didn't tell you the purpose of his visit.'

'His visits, plural. He came twice, three days apart. First, on Tuesday 9 October and then last Friday, the day before his death. I don't know what they discussed but my father didn't seem to enjoy his visits.'

'What did he look like?' asked Fourier more forcefully.

'Sixty, average height, seventy-odd kilos. His nose was hooked, like a beak. He had enormous sideburns and tufts of unkempt sparse white hair that stuck out. He was like an actor in the theatre. But the most striking thing about him was his eyes. They were black, very piercing, and hidden behind ridiculous Chinese glasses with square frames. He was not very nice and that's putting it mildly.'

'Ah! You didn't mention his visits before!'

'I most certainly did! I told one of Second Lieutenant Rouzé's men! He didn't seem very interested.'

Poor Monsieur Rouzé looked as if he would have liked the earth to swallow him up but Monsieur Breteuil unexpectedly came to his rescue.

'We seem to have wandered off the subject, gentlemen. Clearly the German professor didn't go into the Marquis's room and cause his mortal fear.'

'The Sûreté Nationale leaves no stone unturned, sir,' replied Fourier authoritatively. 'All possibilities must be considered, nothing left to chance. You say that he visited twice, Mademoiselle. How did he get here? By car?'

'Yes. Well, the owner of the garage in the village also provides a taxi service when he feels like it. He dropped the professor here and waited in the car.'

'So he was staying nearby. Is the village far?'

'About a mile away.'

'Is there a hotel there?'

'An inn.'

'Raymond, go and have a look round the village. Find out about a foreigner who might have stayed there for several days, just over a week ago.'

Dupuytren hadn't moved a muscle since the start of the interview. It was impossible to tell whether he was miles away or whether, in fact, he had been following every word of what was being said. Hearing his name, he immediately stood to attention.

'At the same time,' added the superintendent, 'try to get hold of the garage owner. And don't dawdle, it's important!'

'Ask my chauffeur to drive you,' interjected Monsieur Breteuil. 'It'll be quicker!'

The constable hurried to the door.

'Didn't Jacques meet this visitor one afternoon as well?' asked the Marquise, looking at her daughter.

'Jacques?' enquired the superintendent.

'Mother, I don't think that really concerns these gentlemen.'

'Who is he?' Fourier insisted

'A young writer interested in my father's work. He's writing a book on dreams in our civilisation, from Antiquity to the present day. That's why he came to the château.'

'Often?'

'Every Friday afternoon for two months!' replied the Marquise. 'He was a considerate boy, charming. And my husband seemed to get on very well with him. When he found out about my husband's death, he immediately came to offer his condolences. He was very upset himself.'

'I don't remember such a visit being mentioned in your report,' the examining magistrate remarked to Second Lieutenant Rouzé, who was sitting opposite him on the other side of the table.

'Well … it didn't seem particularly relevant,' replied the gendarme, sinking further into his armchair.

'Not particularly relevant?' repeated Monsieur Breteuil, twisting his white beard.

Amélie's cheeks had become slightly pink at the mention of Jacques's name.

Not wishing to prolong the young woman's discomfort (but intending to come back to it at a more appropriate moment), I abruptly changed the subject and took the book bound in brown leather that I had found under the Marquis's bed out of my pocket.

'Ladies, does this book mean anything to you?'

The Marquise's brow furrowed.

'It belongs to my husband. He bought it a few years ago. It's been part of his bedtime reading since he began his psychic work.'

'What do you mean?'

'I can't tell you any more. I have never read it and have no intention of doing so.'

'Would you allow me, Madame, to hold on to it for two or three days?'

'Oh! You can keep it if it interests you!'

Thanking her, I put the book back inside my jacket.

'What do you intend to do with the Marquis's papers? He must have written up his research in notebooks. Can they be consulted?'

'I don't see how reading them would help your investigation,' retorted the Marquise.

'In any case, I fear that it will not be possible,' put in Amélie. 'My father wrote on loose sheets of paper which he covered in his small, cramped and almost illegible hand. He himself found it hard to make sense of the muddle. I challenge anyone who is not familiar with his handwriting to decipher anything.'

'So all is lost?' I exclaimed.

'When Dr Osty telephoned on Sunday to offer his condolences, he did indicate that the Institut Métapsychique would like to collect and publish my father's latest work. I offered to put it together. It is true that I am the best person for the job. It will take time, perhaps several months, but I think it should be done.'

The sitting-room door was opened abruptly by Dupuytren, who was supposed to have left a good ten minutes earlier for the village. He had lost his usual composure and seemed out of breath.

Behind him could be glimpsed a tall, slender figure.

'Super— Superintendent! I must speak to you …'

While Raymond stood in the doorway, trying to get his words out in a hollow voice, the stranger stepped past the Sûreté constable into the room.

'What a coincidence!' exclaimed the Marquise, putting an end to

Dupuytren's laboured report. 'We were just talking about you a few minutes ago. But do come in, Jacques, please.'

The newcomer, a dashing, slightly haughty young man of about thirty, wore his brown hair slightly longer than was fashionable.

He looked intently at Amélie, whose face had flushed very prettily, and then came over respectfully to greet the Marquise.

Finally, he turned unexpectedly to Fourier and said without preamble: 'Are you Superintendent Edmond Fourier, from the Sûreté Nationale?'

'I am indeed.'

'Superintendent, it's you I've come to see. My name is Jacques Lacroix. I am a journalist with *Paris-Soir*.'

VI

JACQUES LACROIX PLAYS SHERLOCK TO OUR WATSON

The young servant had drawn up a chair for the journalist and, once the introductions had been made by the extremely urbane examining magistrate, Lacroix placed it between the Marquise's armchair and that of Second Lieutenant Rouzé. Refusing the offer of a cup of tea, he sat with his arms crossed as if to protect himself from the volley of criticism which would no doubt be forthcoming. The young man seemed sure of himself.

I watched Superintendent Fourier out of the corner of my eye. He was mechanically tapping the armrest of his chair, wondering how best to tackle the situation.

But he didn't have long to reflect because, after a few seconds' silence, Lacroix took the initiative.

'It wasn't easy getting into the estate, Superintendent. Fortunately, I intercepted your good constable at the gates. Otherwise, I would have had to wait for hours. The sergeants refused to bring me to you.'

Fourier, who, like me, had noticed Amélie's discomfort earlier when Lacroix's name had been mentioned, acted as if he hadn't heard and addressed the Marquis's daughter.

'Mademoiselle, were you aware that Monsieur Lacroix was the author of the article in Tuesday's *Paris-Soir* that caused such a stir?'

'Well …' mumbled the young lady, embarrassed at the thought of lying in front of her mother.

'Amélie has nothing to do with this!'

'I think you've done enough already, Monsieur Lacroix. Kindly just answer the questions put to you.'

'Excuse me,' said the Marquise in surprise. 'So it was you, Jacques, who wrote that article?'

'Yes, Madame.'

'Why?'

'When I learnt of the Marquis's death I was deeply shaken. I was aware of the details after seeing you on Saturday. It reminded me of what had happened to Pierre Ducros a few months ago. I knew Pierre well. I met him ten years ago when I myself was gravitating towards the circle of Surrealist writers. I was very cut up by his death and the fact that the police, the prosecutor and even his sister, Suzanne, didn't see anything unnatural in it made it even harder for me. When the Marquis was discovered in his bed in identical circumstances I immediately tried to establish a link between the two cases. You didn't need to be a psychic; the chances of two such extraordinary deaths occurring so close together were infinitesimal. And to cap it all, no one else seemed to have noticed the connection. So I had to act alone, and quickly. Given my position, warning the public in an article seemed to be the simplest way. I hoped that by highlighting the inefficiency of the prosecutor's study and the police force, my argument would hit home and the police and justice system would be obliged to reconsider their position. I apologise, gentlemen. My behaviour is certainly not blameless but I didn't have a choice.'

This speech was made with such vigour and sincerity (it was too early to say whether or not it was true) that I sensed Fourier was slightly taken aback. He showed no sign of it though.

'On that point,' declared the superintendent, 'you can be satisfied that you succeeded. I've been asked by my superiors to look into the

Brindillac case myself. As for Ducros, those in a senior position at the Préfecture have been requested to reopen the case. This news isn't common knowledge yet but I imagine that now that you know about it, it may as well already be in the papers.'

'I am delighted, Superintendent. Let's just hope that the Préfecture de Police proves to be more inspired than usual!'

As this dig had been aimed at the Préfecture, Fourier thought it prudent not to respond. I think that secretly he even quite enjoyed it.

'I hope you were right in forcing the justice system to act,' warned the examining magistrate. 'Otherwise, action could be taken against you.'

'I'm only too well aware of that.'

'What was your friend like?' the superintendent went on.

'Pierre was very charming and exceptionally intelligent. I met him at a Surrealist meeting. He had always been very interested in dreams. That's why he wanted to join the group. The great *époque des sommeils* had just ended but dreams continued to occupy a central place in their work. Pierre and I got on very well. He was from the North of France, from a working-class family. He and his sister were not meant to live the life of artists and intellectuals. And yet they held on, almost making a success of their careers. If it hadn't been for that terrible death …'

'And you, Lacroix? What's your story?'

'Unlike Pierre, I've never known poverty. I am the son of an upper middle-class family. My father is a banker at Place des Ternes. After university, I worked for *Lapin Rouge*, a magazine devoted to "literary and artistic modernity". Shortly afterwards, I met some of André Breton's friends when I visited the Studyfor Surrealist Research on Rue de Grenelle. That was in November 1924. I was immediately fascinated by the intellectual energy of the group. For a few years I remained a faithful supporter before distancing myself from them gradually. When I joined *Paris-Soir* I continued to see Pierre, although less frequently. He too had moved away from the Surrealists, being drawn towards an austere kind of solitude that appealed to his melancholy temperament. Dreams had become his main preoccupation and his only source of inspiration.'

'It wasn't very clever of you to vanish after the article was published. My men couldn't track you down, either at the newspaper or at home.'

'I wasn't trying to hide from the police. I was just trying to gather as much information as possible for our investigation.'

'*Our* investigation? Really! You've got a nerve, young man.'

'First, I asked Amélie about any visitors the Marquis had received over the last few weeks. None of them appeared suspicious. There were only faithful friends and colleagues from the Institut Métapsychique. None that is except the unknown professor who came to pester the Marquis de Brindillac twice in the days before his death. I remembered too that I had seen him last Friday, going down the steps as I arrived at the château. His face gave me a strange, unpleasant feeling, an inexplicable sense of uneasiness.'

'Did you ask the Marquis de Brindillac what this man wanted?' asked Monsieur Breteuil.

'Of course. It was the first question I asked when I was shown into the library. He seemed annoyed, afraid, but he didn't reply. He just declared that the man wouldn't be bothering him any more.'

'So, he had been bothering him!'

'Undoubtedly. But how exactly, I don't know. Amélie had noticed that a car driven by a man from the village had dropped the stranger off at the château twice. It seemed reasonable to assume that he had found lodgings at an inn in the area.'

'We had come to the same conclusion,' Fourier agreed. 'That's why I sent my constable to the village to find out. Your brilliant entrance delayed him somewhat but no doubt he'll turn up soon with valuable information.'

'It will be a waste of time, Superintendent. I've already been over everything with a fine-tooth comb.'

'Indeed! And what did you find?'

'The stranger went to the Toison d'Or inn at the end of the village. I was there yesterday afternoon. The manager told me that the fellow had stayed for almost a week and that he only left on Saturday, the day the Marquis was found dead in his room. He described the man as a rather unappealing person who spoke French well but with a strong accent. He had only exchanged the usual pleasantries with him. What the manager remembered most was the man's intense black eyes which held your gaze without wanting to let you go and seemed able to see right inside you. He was apparently a professor in Vienna, Austria. Professor of what he didn't say, but he was here for professional reasons. Why would a Viennese professor come and hole up in a village in Seine-et-Oise? That's what the manager was unable to discover. He had his meals sent up to his room every day and on four separate occasions asked the owner of the nearby garage to drive him somewhere. The manager agreed to let me see the man's room so I went up and searched it thoroughly, without finding anything, unfortunately. But he did give me this.'

Lacroix took a sheet of blue paper from the inside pocket of his jacket and held it out to the superintendent.

'The day he left, at about two o'clock in the afternoon, the dining room was full of weekend visitors. Guests were discussing the mysterious death of the Marquis whose body had been found a few hours before. Unusually, the Austrian was sitting in the dining room, listening to what was being said around him and waiting for Monsieur Lerouge, the owner of the garage, who was going to take him to Étampes station. When he got up, a piece of blue paper fell out of his coat. The manager found it under the chair after he had left. He had no idea what it could mean and, unsure what to do, kept it, thinking that the stranger might want it back.'

It was a telegram and care had been taken to remove information relating to the sender and the person it was addressed to. It contained a short three-line message written in German.

'What does it mean?' asked Fourier, giving it back to the journalist.

'There's a translation on the back: "We have chosen new breeders. Confirmation birth 1 expected on 23rd. Awaiting your return to participate in great work."'

'"Breeders!" "Birth!" What does it mean?' asked the examining magistrate, becoming agitated. 'Is your man a professor or a vet? And the twenty-third of what? October?'

'I don't know yet.'

'With luck, it will have come via the local post office,' Fourier observed. 'They'll be able to help us.'

'I've already checked. The stranger neither received nor sent any telegrams while he was staying in the area.'

'By the way, what name did he use at La Toison d'Or?' I asked after I had copied the message into my dream notebook.

'Hans-Rudolf von Öberlin.'

'Very good!' announced Monsieur Breteuil. 'This is all very troubling, I grant you, but there's not a shred of evidence to implicate this person in the death of the Marquis de Brindillac.'

'That's true,' said Lacroix, glancing at Amélie. 'This morning I also met Suzanne Ducros to find out if this strange Austrian had visited Pierre as well.'

'And?'

'Well, she remembered an old, stooped man with dull white hair under a top hat. He was wearing a long black coat and round glasses.

His general appearance was almost grotesque. According to her description, he looked like Dr Caligari.'

'Cagliari?' repeated the magistrate.

'Caligari,' I said, 'was a Machiavellian character in a German silent film that came out about fifteen years ago.'

'Suzanne remembered his eyes most: intense, black, they looked straight into your very soul. This man had met Pierre two or three days before he died. She didn't know if he was a professor but he spoke with a German accent.'

'Why did he want to see Ducros?'

'She didn't know. Her brother had deliberately stayed silent on the subject. She only remembered his name: Andreas Eberlin. *Eberlin! Öberlin!* Not much imagination.'

'Your description of this man doesn't correspond to the one given by the young lady earlier!' said Monsieur Breteuil irritably. 'This one doesn't have sideburns or a hooked nose. And his glasses are round ...'

'Props!' objected Fourier. 'Nothing could be simpler than transforming his face with a false beard and a white wig. As for the glasses, well, come on! The most important thing is the similarities between the two descriptions: the German accent and the terrible eyes.'

'I saw those eyes on the steps of the château,' recalled the journalist. 'They are unforgettable, I can attest to that. In any case, I am certain, absolutely certain, you understand, that it's the same man.'

'All right, all right,' said the magistrate, who was not one to get carried away.

'You admit that it would be truly amazing if it was just a coincidence.'

'Certainly,' granted Fourier. 'But as Monsieur Breteuil said earlier, it doesn't make this man a killer. After all, Lacroix, you knew both victims as well.'

'You're right. I too am officially a suspect. But please, Superintendent, don't ignore the Austrian because of that.'

'Our young friend has nothing to do with my husband's death!' cried the Marquise. 'And, gentlemen, would you kindly see fit to explain your thinking? As far as I know, no one killed the Marquis de Brindillac. How could the man you're talking about, or anyone else, be accused of anything?'

'For the moment, Madame, no one is guilty of anything in this affair,' replied Fourier. 'And that is the problem. We're trying to understand how it is possible for two men to die of fright in their sleep, in order to prevent such a tragedy occurring again.'

'If we don't want it to happen again,' Lacroix cried, 'this man must be found! He must have something to do with these events!'

Judge Breteuil, seeing that the Marquise was showing signs of agitation, hastened to bring the interview to a close.

'I think that the investigation now has some new information. Everything must be done to find out as much as possible about this individual. In the meantime, I propose that we end the meeting here and let the Marquise return to her duties.'

Although the magistrate had already risen, I felt it necessary to clarify one last point.

'Monsieur Lacroix! You reported that the garage owner had driven the stranger on four occasions. He came here to the château twice and was taken to Étampes station on Saturday. That makes three journeys. Do you know the destination of the fourth journey?'

'Ah, yes, thank you! I had forgotten about my visit to Monsieur Lerouge. I didn't count the journey to the station in my calculations. So that makes five journeys in total, including two to the northern districts of Paris. Unfortunately, the garage owner doesn't remember the dates of those two trips. He simply told me that the Austrian had paid him in cash on the spot and that, that being the case, he would have liked the gentleman to visit the capital more often.'

'Where did he go on those trips?'

'The first was to 89 Avenue Niel. The second was to Montmartre.'

'Eighty-nine Avenue Niel? Isn't that the address of the headquarters of the Institut Métapsychique International?

'That's right.'

'What did he do there?'

'I have no idea for the moment. According to Monsieur Lerouge, he stayed for half an hour. Afterwards, he returned to La Toison d'Or.'

'And Montmartre?'

'The garage owner dropped him off at the end of the afternoon on the corner of Rue Fontaine and Boulevard de Clichy. He noticed that the man went into a café and only came out at about quarter to eight.'

'A café?' exclaimed Fourier.

'Yes, Café de la Place Blanche.'

'Was he thirsty then?'

'I don't know, Superintendent. But it is common knowledge that the Surrealists have been using that brasserie as their new headquarters ever since they were forced to abandon the Cyrano. André Breton's group meets there every evening between half past six and half past seven.'

VII

I WIN TWO CASES OF VOUVRAY

The case had moved on apace in the space of a few hours. Lacroix's information still had to be verified though.

When Dupuytren returned, he more or less confirmed what the journalist had said. A certain Hans-Rudolf von Öberlin had stayed at La Toison d'Or for six days until Saturday 13 October, the day the Marquis de Brindillac had died. Having been informed about the man who had provided a taxi service for the Austrian professor, Dupuytren had then gone to see the garage owner, who had told him about the five journeys he had made.

Now it was a question of picking up the trail of the mysterious stranger and that didn't look as if it would be straightforward. Of the two names he had used it was unlikely that either was his real name. And despite the details we had of his appearance, there was nothing definite to hold on to. The stranger seemed to take a mischievous pleasure in disguising himself – with the exception of those remarkably intense eyes which made such an impression on everyone who saw them. To top it all, there was nothing to confirm that the man was still in Paris.

There was no need for us to remain at the château any longer. Given the late hour, the superintendent made sure he telephoned headquarters before we left to request that two of his men should go immediately to the Café de la Place Blanche and stayed there until he arrived. The Austrian might be spotted again and Fourier passed on the description provided by Amélie and Suzanne Ducros.

It also seemed imperative to visit the Institut Métapsychique International as soon as possible. If the man had spoken to Charles Richet, Dr Osty or any other eminent members of the society, we might get some more information from them.

What connected the Austrian to the metapsychists and Surrealists? It was a question that needed answering as soon as possible.

Jacques Lacroix offered us a lift back to Paris in his car, which was parked not far from the château grounds. As we still had some questions for him, we gladly accepted and took our leave of the Marquise and her daughter, as well as the examining magistrate and the clerk, before proceeding to the gates where the gendarmes, on the orders of Second Lieutenant Rouzé, were now doing their utmost to prevent journalists and the curious approaching the château.

The sun was low in the sky as the engine of the red Peugeot Torpedo sputtered into life.

I used the bumpy journey (and bumpy is the word; the exessively tight suspension sent me flying up to the canvas roof over and over again) to ask Lacroix to explain exactly what the Marquis de Brindillac had been working on.

After decades spent studying sleep according to the most rigorous rules of physiology, the scientist's ideas had been shaken by his growing awareness, through Professor Richet and his associates at the Institut Métapsychique, of the work of a certain Frederik Willem Van Eeden, a Dutch psychiatrist who had methodically recorded the contents of his dreams for twenty years. In 1913 he had noticed that, during certain dreams, he remained perfectly aware that he was in the process of dreaming. He had described that mental state in an article for the Proceedings of the Society for Psychical Research (SPR). During a so-called lucid dream, the cognitive faculties are not suspended; the sleeper experiences the dream very intensely, gliding through a dream-like world which seems surprisingly real, while still being able to reason with clarity and even remember his waking life. As he has almost total control of the dream, he can transform it at will, make characters appear or disappear, act according to plans drawn up in advance, defy the laws of nature, fly and pass through matter.

In truth, Frederik Van Eeden didn't discover lucid dreams. Aristotle and Descartes had recounted their brief experiences of this kind. In particular, in 1867 a French orientalist, Hervey de Saint-Denys, had discussed the subject in a book which had gone unnoticed at the time, *Les Rêves et les moyens de les diriger* (Dreams and How to Control Them). However, since Hervey, no serious work had been carried out and, with the exception of Van Eeden's article, lucid dreams had been almost completely forgotten.

The Marquis de Brindillac had also scrupulously recorded thousands of his dreams in his notebooks. Some were undeniably in the lucid category. From the day he had made this discovery, Brindillac had devoted all his energy to studying and elucidating this strange state of mind.

Despite repeated attempts, Lacroix had been unable to discover the precise stage the scientist had reached in his work. However, he must have obtained some results because the directors of the Institut had been planning to organise a lecture before the end of the year, to which Europe's leading experts in psychic research would have been invited.

'Which makes a visit to these gentlemen even more necessary,' declared Fourier, who was sitting in the front seat.

'Yes. And I wonder what the Marquis was intending to tell them all.'

'I don't know,' said Lacroix. 'But knowing him, it must have been damned important.'

A hole in the road bounced me up to the ceiling again and, as I fell back on to the narrow seat, I almost crushed the book I'd taken from the château.

'By the way,' I continued, 'earlier, we found a book under the Marquis's bed. It's called *Le Comte de Gabalis or Discourses on the Secret Sciences*.'

'Yes, I noticed it once or twice among the pile of books on his desk.'

'I'm sure I've seen the title somewhere before but I've racked my brains and I can't remember where. On the inside cover it says it was written in 1670.'

'By a certain Abbé Montfaucon de Villars, yes. A strange fellow, that one! After a career as a cadet of Gascony, he made a name for himself as a literary adventurer in Paris before being mixed up in a dark vendetta, for which he and his accomplices were sentenced to be broken on the wheel. But the Abbé obviously managed to escape that fate because he died a few years later, his throat cut by outlaws on the road to Lyons.'

'Ah! The roads were much more dangerous than today,' growled Fourier as a bend negotiated at full speed almost sent us into a ditch. 'Would it be too much to ask, Lacroix, for you to drive more slowly?'

'Apologies, Superintendent. To return to Abbé de Villars, jokers spread the rumour that ethereal spirits killed him to punish him for revealing the mysteries of the secret sciences to the general public.'

'Ethereal spirits?'

'That's what the book is about actually. The main character, Gabalis, is a Hermetic philosopher and he explains to his follower Rosicrucian theories on the existence and powers of sylphs, gnomes and other elemental spirits that fill the atmosphere. According to him, it is possible for man to enter into contact with these entities, which are invisible to the naked eye, and, in certain conditions, bond with their females. The possibility of this kind of union has allegedly been proven since the dawn of time, and most of humanity's heroes through the ages (Solomon, Zoroaster, Achilles, Hercules, Aeneas, Plato, Merlin and so on) are actually the offspring of these unusual love affairs. As you can imagine, after its publication the book was banned. The Church also banned the author from the pulpit because it couldn't establish whether the Abbé was just having some fun or whether he was actually serious.'

Superintendent Fourier burst out laughing. 'Well, maybe Brindillac was trying to create one of these carnal unions then! If that's the case, I take my hat off to him. What energy at his age!'

'I don't know why the Marquis was interested in *Le Comte de Gabalis* actually. To the best of my knowledge, he had no particular liking for light-hearted books.'

I lit a cigarette to distract myself from the damned car's suspension. Next to me, Dupuytren appeared to be quietly enjoying my ordeal.

Fortunately, the signposts which were lit up every now and then by the Torpedo's headlights told us that we would soon be in Paris.

'You seem to know a lot about this book yourself, Monsieur Lacroix.'

'Let's just say that it's one of the set texts for the apprentice Surrealist. Traditionally, the elemental entities in question are related to the incubi and succubi which have always tormented sleepers. I've devoted a chapter to them in the book I'm writing on the representation of dreams in our society.'

'Incubi? Succubi? What are they?'

'Nocturnal creatures,' I explained. 'The ancient treatises on demonology are riddled with tales of men and women who were victims of their attacks at night while they were asleep[11]. But I admit that I don't quite see the connection with the Surrealists.'

'Well, succubi were the subject of numerous discussions at group meetings a few years ago. Some members have written very eloquently on this theme[12]. In a report about sexuality, published in 1928 in *La Révolution surréaliste*, some even considered carnal relations with a succubus to be one of the most intense pleasures known to man.'

'Were they speaking from first-hand knowledge?'

'To be frank, Monsieur Singleton, succubi were really a literary creation and none of them seriously believed in the existence of immaterial unions. Breton, for example, reduced the subject to a simple psychological phenomenon.'

'Your friend Pierre Ducros, had he read *Le Comte de Gabalis*?'

'I can't be sure but it seems likely that he did.'

By the light of the streetlamps I recognised the familiar outlines of Haussmann buildings and boulevards. My ordeal was nearly at an end.

'To return to the Surrealists,' I began, just as we drove on to a long paved stretch of Avenue d'Italie, crushing my hopes, 'you mentioned the *époque des sommeils* this afternoon. I recall Breton referring to it at the beginning of *Nadja*. What is it?'

'Have you read *Nadja*? My word, you're the first Englishman I've met to do so.'

'I'm not English, I'm Canadian. From Halifax in Nova Scotia.'

'Maybe so, but that doesn't alter the scale of the achievement. As for the *époque des sommeils*, it was one of the most exciting periods! Right at the beginning of the movement, when most of the members were about twenty-five, they carried out a crucial experiment which completely changed how they viewed reality. During the summer holidays of 1922, René Crevel took part in a spiritualist séance organised by a certain Madame Dante. Very quickly, he fell into a deep sleep during which, according to the other participants, he said some remarkable words. Upon his return, Crevel shared his experience with other members of the group and Breton suggested repeating the séance in his studio. Crevel and Breton were joined by Max Morise, Simone, André's partner at the time, and Robert Desnos, a new member of the circle. Crevel followed the same protocol as the medium: he turned off the lights, requested silence and invited the group to hold hands in a circle around the table. After a few minutes, Crevel fell into a deep sleep and, in a state of trance, began to recount a wonderful tale which rivalled the most horrifying pages of the *Chants de Maldoror*. A few days later it was Desnos's turn to fall into a hypnotic trance and answer questions, incongruously and poetically, in writing. At the end of the séance he improvised a sonnet. Breton was naturally astounded at the evocative power of hypnotic sleep. After the discovery of "automatic writing" and his work on dream narratives, he was convinced he had uncovered a new vein of creativity. As far as he was concerned, access to the source of poetry itself had just been found. The séances continued at a frenzied rate. It was at that time that I heard of the Surrealists. I must have been about eighteen. But when I finally met them two years later at their headquarters in Rue de Grenelle, the famous *époque des sommeils* was over. Breton had decided to stop in February 1923.'

'Why? Did the well dry up?'

'For the simple reason that it was becoming impossible to control the séances. You know, a state of trance brings out certain aspects of character which are not necessarily fit to be seen. Some members began to argue violently and, above all, display aggressive behaviour. There were insults, frightening predictions, punches thrown, etc. It totally degenerated. I was told that, during a meeting organised at Marie de La Hire's home near Place de Clichy, no fewer than ten people went into a trance at the same time. By common agreement, with a rope around their necks, they decided to hang themselves from the coat stands. They had to be woken up with slaps and glasses of cold water thrown in their faces. And of course, it must not be forgotten that Breton is a committed materialist deep down. Yes, he adopted some spiritualist techniques for his trance sessions but he has always categorically rejected the idea of communication between the world of the living and that of the dead.'

We had passed the Palais de Justice and crossed the Seine via the ancient Pont-au-Change. Fourier, who was starting to become irritated with our literary chatter, considering it unsuitable for advancing a police investigation, decided to change the subject.

'So, Lacroix! You seem to get on very well with the Marquis's daughter. What is your relationship with her?'

'What do you mean, Superintendent?' replied the journalist, pretending to be offended. 'Mademoiselle Amélie is a very nice person but I can assure you that our relations are based purely on courtesy.'

We had just passed the Théâtre des Nations when, fifty yards further on, I caught sight of a huge figure I would have recognised anywhere.

'Hey! Pull over, will you! I think I've just won two cases of Vouvray!'

The journalist, not sorry that the conversation had taken a new turn, braked sharply and parked on Avenue Victoria.

Having extricated myself from the car with great relief, my muscles aching, I called out to my faithful friend, who was walking along the pavement of Square Saint-Jacques with his hands in his pockets.

'Well, at last!' cried James, spinning round at the sound of my voice.

Then, noticing the superintendent, his constable and the

journalist, who had followed me out of the car, he continued in the language of Molière: 'How are you, Superintendent? I've been wandering around this area for two hours, waiting for you to get here. I had time to devour a plate of leg of lamb and two helpings of a succulent strawberry charlotte. Actually, I was wondering if I should go back for more.'

We had joined my friend on the other side of the avenue and formed a small group in the circle of light cast by a streetlamp, close to the park railings. Above our heads, a three-quarter moon shone over the statue of Saint Jacques le Majeur.

It was eight o'clock in the evening according to my pocket watch. We were standing at almost exactly the spot where Rue de la Vieille-Lanterne had begun eighty years earlier.

James seemed to be in a good mood, as he always was when he picked up the scent of a sensational case.

'Just one question. The case you referred to in your telegram hasn't been solved yet, has it?'

'Of course not, far from it, my friend,' said the superintendent.

'Good. I wouldn't want to miss it for the world! When I received your message, Andrew, I rushed over to the reading room of the British Museum to find a copy of *Paris-Soir*.'

'About that,' I said, gesturing towards Jacques Lacroix, 'you have before you the brilliant author of the article.'

'Better and better! And, gentlemen, I think I've brought you something new!'

With a flourish, he produced from his pocket a page neatly clipped from a newspaper and began to unfold it slowly in order to prolong the pleasure.

'This is an extract from the *Daily Gazette* from 7 June. The news only merited a small paragraph but it's worth its weight in gold. Listen to this:

'On Monday night (4 June) Percival Crowles of South Audley Street near Hyde Park, one of the most brilliant doctors at the neurological hospital in Queen Square, London, died in his sleep at his home. It appears that his heart stopped suddenly as if in the grip of a night terror. The doctor was found dead the following day by a housekeeper engaged in his service. Percival Crowles was a recognised specialist in sleep disorders, particularly narcolepsy. Originally from Southampton, he read medicine at University College before … blah blah blah.

Queen Square hospital is a stone's throw from our rooms in Montague Street,' continued James, folding up the article. 'Yesterday evening, after leaving the British Museum where I had consulted the copy of *Paris-Soir*, I went to have a drink at McInnes's and filled him in on this case of Deadly Sleep. It was he who alerted me to the death of the doctor from Queen Square in the spring. He remembered because nurses from the neurological hospital drink in his pub and they had talked about it a lot at the time. This morning, before catching the train, I returned to the reading room and got hold of this article from June. So, what do you say?'

'Good heavens!' exclaimed Fourier. 'It's a veritable epidemic!'

'I'm going to Rue du Louvre straight away,' declared the journalist. 'If need be, I'll spend the whole night in the archives combing through the international press. We must find out if there have been other cases in the past few months. Can I drop you off somewhere, Superintendent?'

'No, get off to your archives! I'll take a taxi to Place Blanche. With luck, my men at the Surrealists' brasserie will have good news. Then I'll go back to headquarters to contact the Viennese police. This Öberlin (or Eberlin) may be known to them. I suggest we meet tomorrow at Hôtel Saint-Merri, Rue de la Verrerie, to take stock of the situation. Eleven o'clock sharp!'

The journalist shook our hands and ran to his car.

'One more thing!' cried Fourier. 'Please don't say anything about all this in your damned paper, Lacroix! We must be as discreet as possible. Understood?'

'Don't worry, Superintendent. My lips are sealed.'

Then he leapt into the Torpedo.

'And I thought I'd arrived after the battle,' James congratulated himself. 'But someone must explain it all to me – the Surrealists, Vienna, Öberlin …'

'Come on,' I said, taking him by the shoulder. 'I'll explain everything.'

VIII

TOO MUCH READING CAN DAMAGE
YOUR SLEEP

We spent most of the evening sitting outside a brasserie on Rue Saint-Martin, sipping glasses of Dubonnet. As promised, I brought James up to date with the details of Superintendent Fourier's investigation.

'What's your feeling about this case, Andrew?' he asked when I'd finished. 'Do you really think this Öberlin fellow had anything to do with those deaths?'

'It's just supposition at the moment. The fact that this strange Austrian professor—'

'But is he a professor? Is he even Austrian?' James interrupted.

'We don't know anything for certain. Anyway, the fact that this person met both victims—'

'Because you're convinced that the men who visited the Marquis and the poet a few days before they died were one and the same person?'

'It's one of the few leads we've got. We have no choice but to follow it up.'

'What about Jacques Lacroix? As the superintendent said, he was in touch with Ducros and the Marquis as well. Do you think he's in the clear?'

'If he had had anything to do with the Austrian, why would he have written that article in *Paris-Soir*? After all, it's thanks to him that we know the two cases are connected.'

'Hmm! If it were the same visitor and if we can show that he also tried to see Percival Crowles, the doctor from Queen Square hospital, that really would change things. It's a pity I'm not in London to investigate.'

'A pity indeed,' I agreed, drawing greedily on my Turkish cigarette.

'This fellow may also simply have wanted to meet them to warn them of danger. If that's the case, then he's a good Samaritan!'

'But remember that neither the Marquis de Brindillac nor Pierre Ducros seemed to be thrilled to see him.'

'Yes, but that doesn't mean he's guilty, does it? And, of course, they might have died of natural causes. There's still everything to prove in that respect.'

'True, frightening someone to death in their sleep isn't yet on the statute book.'

'Fine, so to sum up: on the one hand, we have two victims (three now), and possibly more in the future, with no actual proof of foul play, and the only thing the victims share is their interest in sleep and dreams. On the other hand, we have an untraceable suspect whose guilt has yet to be proved.'

'Exactly, James! An excellent summary!'

'You said earlier that the Austrian was one of the few leads we've got. As far as I can see, it's the only one. We must find this fellow.'

'There is a second lead which you just mentioned.'

'What?'

'The victims' interest in sleep and dreams, be it scientific or artistic. I'm convinced it plays a crucial role in this case.'

'Maybe Fourier was right to talk in terms of an epidemic. Could it be a new form of bacteria which has suddenly appeared and has a fatal effect while you're dreaming? Great sleepers like me and vivid dreamers like you, Andrew, should beware.'

'The *Bacillus somnii*!' I added, amused by this theory.

My partner stretched his arms above his head, yawning, and drained his glass of Dubonnet in one gulp.

'I don't know about you but I'm exhausted. Tomorrow will be a long and fascinating day. I think I'll defy our *Bacillus* now and get my strength back.'

'I have absolutely no desire to go to bed myself,' I replied, lighting another cigarette. 'I think I'll go for a walk. See you tomorrow, James.'

I went to bed very late that night. Wishing to clear my head from the effects of alcohol and lack of sleep, I strolled leisurely past the Louvre, Place Vendôme and up to the area around Opéra, where I caught the last omnibus back.

I wanted to delay the moment of sleep for as long as possible. All evening we had speculated about the inexplicable deaths of the Marquis de Brindillac, Pierre Ducros and Percival Crowles. Such a gloomy discussion about so-called Deadly Sleep certainly did not encourage one to slip into the arms of Morpheus.

But that was not the only reason. I had not thought about the previous night's dream since recording it in my notebook that morning before joining Fourier at the Gare d'Orsay. It had completely slipped my mind. As I returned to my room it suddenly came flooding back.

In all my life I had never had a dream that was so vivid or so acutely realistic, leaving me so confused upon waking. I had been too busy to think about it during the day. Yet there was much to ponder. During the dream I had had a feeling of singularly intense emotion, of sexual excitement towards the unknown young woman, and part of me wanted to feel that emotion and that excitement again. Another part vigorously rejected it. If she truly existed (something I was beginning to doubt; my memory of our meeting on the steamer had taken on the quality of a dream), I felt guilty about entertaining such feelings.

Was I not unwillingly a bit like the incubi Lacroix and I had discussed earlier? And did this not indicate that those tales of immaterial unions were nothing more than vague repressed desires?

A bottomless chasm was opening beneath me, filled with my frustrations, obsessions and weaknesses.

The hotel was relatively quiet at that time of year so James had been given the room next to mine. I could hear him snoring as I passed his door.

Despite my tiredness, I found it very difficult to fall asleep. I had brushed aside the memory of my dream but reason would not surrender so easily. I kept going over the events of the day in my head. One point in particular continued to intrigue me. I was convinced that I had recently come across a reference to *Le Comte de Gabalis* or its author. And at that moment I thought I remembered where.

Impatient to settle the matter, I turned the bedside light on again and picked up one of the volumes of the complete works of Gérard de Nerval which included *Les Illuminés*. This was a collection of disparate texts in which the writer outlined his favourite eccentrics, characters both impassioned and inclined to dreaming. The fifth was dedicated to Jacques Cazotte, an author from the eighteenth century who was remembered for a delightful novel, *Le Diable amoureux*, which had been inspired (as Nerval noted) by a book written a hundred years before by a certain Abbé Montfaucon de Villars: *Le Comte de Gabalis*. What is more, I found the anecdote Jacques Lacroix had mentioned about Villars's death.

I now remembered reading *Le Diable amoureux* a few years earlier. It was a half-mischievous, half-serious book about the adventures of a young officer in the king's guard in Naples who, after a bet with his regimental comrades about the alleged powers of the cabbala, tried to invoke the occult forces of nature one evening in the ruins at Portici. A terrifying ghost that looked like a camel's head appeared and then revealed itself to be a gracious sylph-like creature prepared to grant all his wishes. At the end of the tale the author, lapsing into tragedy, intimated that it was the devil in person who had taken on female form the better to trick the young officer.

Later in the article, there was a brief digression on the nature of these elemental spirits. Eusèbe, Saint Augustine, Cazotte and Abbé de Villars were convinced they existed in a state of perfect innocence from the Christian point of view.

I closed the book and, wanting to find out more about *Le Comte de Gabalis*, picked up the 1921 edition I had found at Château B—. I read all five discourses (it was only about a hundred pages long) and flicked through the commentary which accompanied them as well.

Jacques Lacroix had summarised the book accurately. The discourses of Gabalis, a German lord and famous occultist, reported by one of his French disciples, covered the existence of 'elementals' and the means of contacting them.

According to the Count of Gabalis, many races, whose women and girls are formidably beautiful, inhabit the four elements which make up the universe: sylphs and sylphids fill the air, fire teems with salamanders, the rivers and the seas are home to water sprites and nymphs, and the centre of the earth contains male and female gnomes. When the world was created, Adam, made from what was purest in the elements, was the natural king of these creatures, who appeared proud but were actually docile and devoted to their master. However, after his sin deprived him of his throne and corrupted the principles from which he had been created, he lost sovereignty over the invisible peoples. Only a philosopher, whose bodily form had been regenerated and exalted through the assiduous study of the secret sciences, would be able to establish communication with them again.

That being so, the Count of Gabalis did not conceal the fact that he had renounced the charms of human females in order to devote himself exclusively to his invisible mistresses and their delectable embraces.

Cazotte, Abbé de Villars, the Count of Gabalis, elemental spirits, sensual cabbalistic pleasures ... After more than two hours of attentive reading, a feeling of mellow drowsiness eventually stole over me. I put the book on the chair and drifted off almost immediately.

In the confusion of my initial nocturnal visions – the ones which appear as soon as the brain gently succumbs to sleep – it crossed my mind that I had left my dream notebook in my jacket. I didn't have the energy to get up though, so the book remained where it was.

As I expected, as I both hoped and feared with the same intensity, I woke up in the middle of the night, shaken by a new dream.

DREAM 2
NIGHT OF 18–19 OCTOBER

Bedtime: 12.25 a.m.
Approximate time when fell asleep: 2.20 a.m.
Time awoken: 3.55 a.m.

I am stretched out on my bed in my room at the Hôtel Saint-Merri and I am dreaming that I am asleep. Like last night, I dream while fully aware that I am dreaming.

I know that the stranger from the steamer will join me soon. She promised; it's inevitable. In the meantime, I sleep peacefully. My dreams are connected to events of the day, the visit to Château B— with Superintendent Fourier, the investigation into the death of the Marquis, James's arrival in Paris. While dreaming, I hear myself telling myself that these are just memories from my daytime existence because, in reality, I am dreaming.

Suddenly, I sense that the door has just opened and someone has entered the room. It is her, I'm sure of it. I open my eyes slowly, without experiencing the slightly dazed feeling one normally has on waking, as if there were no difference between sleep and the reality before me.

It is her, the young woman from the steamer, wearing a fine red satin dress which shows off the delicate outline of her hips and chest perfectly. Her blond hair floats in the air as she approaches the bed, smiling. She gives off a sort of phosphorescence which glows all around her.

She sits on the edge of my bed and, in the same movement, her alluring lips touch mine. Her skin is soft, like the softest silk.

Then I hear her whisper, 'Do you remember Fata Morgana*? You must remember.'*

Before I can answer, she moves her face away and looks at me intensely as if feeling sudden anxiety.

'Dark forces are preparing to turn the world upside down. I am afraid for you, Andrew. You must believe in me – your life depends on it.'

'What forces? What are you talking about?'

Her expression hardens suddenly.

I want to keep hold of her because I feel that she is going to escape again. I would like her to stay so much! While raising her hand to tell me to be quiet, she rises and glides towards the chair, takes my dream notebook out of my jacket and, seeming to float above the floor, places it at the foot of the bed.

Then, just like the day before and despite my desire, despite my disappointment, she moves away towards the door, pointing at the book.

When the door closes, I wake up with a start.

NOTES UPON WAKING

1. When I opened my eyes I only had to reach out my arm to pick up my notebook at the end of the bed. What am I to make of it? Could it be that, knowing I would need it, I had placed it there automatically before going to bed? Was everything else just my mind playing tricks on me?

2. I feel feverish and nervous. I still have the taste of her lips on mine. I can smell the fragrance of her skin, feel the softness of her caresses on my body. How can a simple dream seem so real? I fear that sleep has abandoned me for the rest of the night.

IX

AN OMINOUS INCREASE IN THE
NUMBER OF CASES

My cigarette-holder hung from my lips. I had been engrossed in the biography of Nerval all morning.

It had been impossible to go back to sleep after my dream. In vain I had hoped for a few more hours' rest but I abandoned my bed in desperation as soon as the first rays of the sun appeared. After a frugal meal for which I had no appetite, I dreaded returning to a room in which my mind had demonstrated an excessive tendency to dream so I sat at one of the hotel's reading tables near the lobby.

'Oh, what I wouldn't give just to have a quick look at that damned police file!' I exclaimed, looking up at the reception desk.

'I fear that you'll have to give up that idea,' replied a familiar voice from over my shoulder. 'The file was destroyed by the Communards in a fire in 1871, as was part of the Préfecture's archives.'

Jacques Lacroix was standing behind me.

'Nerval's death is a subject for endless speculation,' he continued, 'and that biography you're reading, by Aristide Marie, is fairly well researched.'

'"Fairly well" is somewhat qualified, isn't it?'

'Actually, there are several contradictory versions of events. For example, the theory that Nerval was still alive when he was cut down from the rope by the policeman is at odds with another, not mentioned in the biography, according to which his body had been lifeless for a long time.'

'Ha! It's definitely hard to get to the bottom of what happened. But do I take it that you're interested in Nerval's death?'

'He was the model poet for the Surrealists. In the First Manifesto Breton wrote that "Nerval possessed to a marvellous degree that spirit with which we claim kinship". Although I am no longer a member of the group, I still share many cultural references with them.'

'Yes, I remember Monsieur Breton's homage. Before opting for "Surrealism" as a name, he almost chose "Supernaturalism" – in reference, of course, to *Les Filles du feu*.'

'Monsieur Singleton, your knowledge of French literature is absolutely amazing. A literary detective, it's certainly original.'

'*In libris est verum*. I simply apply this adage and extend the principle to the art of investigation.'

'Well, as I'm dealing with a connoisseur, and to return to Nerval's death, I would like to tell you a secret, my friend. A few years ago, I had an adventure that was quite incredible, even surreal, one might say. It was late afternoon and I was climbing up to the top of Tour Saint-Jacques when a peculiar character approached me. He claimed to have followed the investigation into the tragedy at Rue de la Vieille-Lanterne closely. He even said that he had been involved in some way. The poet had been dead for nearly seventy years by then and, frankly, the stranger didn't look that decrepit. I thought he was pulling my leg. But later I checked the papers from February and March 1855 in detail and I had to admit that most of what he'd told me was true.'

Needless to say, I was finding it very difficult to take the journalist seriously.

'Do you think he was some mad literary historian?' was all I said.

Lacroix laughed. 'Possibly. Anyway, before disappearing, this man entrusted me with a document which would greatly interest you. If we manage to solve our case, I promise I'll show it to you.'

There was a hint of irony in his smile. A new document? Handed over by a stranger at the top of Tour Saint-Jacques? Whatever next! Lacroix must be making fun of me.

'It's almost time for our meeting,' I said, changing the subject.

I compared my pocket watch with the Swiss clock behind the reception desk. My watch was three minutes faster.

'Yes. Actually, I think our friend Fourier is just arriving. Is your partner not here yet?'

'James is not an early riser but he should be here soon. Yes, that must be him I can hear on the stairs.'

Looking dashing in a pale linen suit, James came down the last step just as Superintendent Fourier pushed open the hotel's glass doors.

'Gentlemen!' my associate said brightly. 'Good morning! Superintendent, I recognised your bowler hat from the window of my room. But what has happened to your bodyguard?'

'He is at the Café de la Place Blanche,' replied Fourier. 'He and another of my men are under orders to take it in turns to watch the place all day.'

'Did yesterday's surveillance of the Surrealists' headquarters yield anything?' asked Lacroix.

While James and the journalist had each grabbed a chair and sat down next to me, Fourier was clearly reluctant to sit. He took off his hat and, holding it in his left hand, smoothed the long solitary lock of hair on top of his head with the other hand.

'When I met them last night at the brasserie, my officers indicated that at about half past seven they had seen an individual who appeared to match the description provided by Suzanne Ducros.'

'Suzanne Ducros?' repeated Lacroix, who could not believe his ears.

'Yes. He had all the grotesque features she described to you: top hat, long, dull white hair, round glasses and a wooden cane. He was sitting nursing a glass of beer, not far from Breton and his friends.'

'Well! That completely confirms my theory! Hans-Rudolf von Öberlin and Andreas Eberlin are the same person. I don't know why but it seems our man has swapped the get-up of the first character for the second.'

Lacroix's face suddenly darkened and he looked at the superintendent with abrupt concern.

'Was he in the brasserie when you joined your men? Did you see him?'

'Good heavens, no, it was after half past eight when I arrived. The man had left nearly an hour earlier.'

'What?!' the journalist croaked. 'Your men didn't follow him?'

Fourier decided that the time had come to sit down. He put his hat in front of him on the table and squirmed on his seat.

'Well ... they tried. One of my men decided to follow him while his colleague stayed inside, just in case, to watch the meeting. And ...'

'And?'

'Well, a group of customers came in just as the suspect was leaving and by the time my officer finally managed to get out of the door there was no one there. He waited in the middle of Place Blanche where he had the best view but it was impossible to tell which way the suspect had gone. Rue Blanche? Rue Fontaine? Boulevard de Clichy? Rue Lepic?'

Jacques Lacroix said nothing but you only had to look at him to know that he was silently fuming at the police and their hopeless incompetence.

'Well, there's nothing to prove that he was the man we're looking for,' said James soothingly. 'Maybe it was just a little old man from the area who hurried off to his flat in the building next door.'

'According to my men, the fellow seemed interested in the Surrealists. He was paying them *a lot* of attention.'

'Unless I'm mistaken,' James continued, 'some of these writers and artists are fairly well known in Paris. It's hardly surprising that customers are curious.'

'That's true,' I said. 'A curious customer but who, let me remind you, exactly fits the description provided by Mademoiselle Ducros!'

'It's clear that it was our man,' declared Lacroix. 'And I suppose at least we've learnt that he is probably still in Paris as we speak!'

'Were your men spotted?' I asked.

'I'm sure they weren't!'

'I say!' exclaimed my friend. 'If this fellow really is the Marquis de Brindillac's and Pierre Ducros's unknown visitor, what was he doing in the brasserie? If he is trying to find out about the Surrealists, why not just contact them directly?'

'Maybe he has. In any case, if it's our man, he will probably go back to the Café de la Place Blanche. Either today or another day.'

'Which is why my men are still watching the place.'

I lit another cigarette.

'However, if you'll allow me, Superintendent, Lacroix is the only one of us who has seen Öberlin before. Even if he uses another disguise, our friend would still be able to identify him. If you agree, Superintendent (and if Monsieur Lacroix agrees, of course), I think that his presence at the brasserie would be very helpful.'

'Of course I agree! That goes without saying!'

The reporter had recovered his usual enthusiasm and, with a broad smile, he took a notebook from the inside pocket of his jacket.

'I have not been idle since yesterday, gentlemen. Until four o'clock this morning I was in the *Paris-Soir* archives. A researcher friend of mine helped me. Together, we went through hundreds of newspapers with a fine-tooth comb.'

'And what did you find?'

The journalist flicked through the pages of his notebook.

'I found two cases which are very similar to ours. One in Amsterdam, the other in New York. Amsterdam first: on 9 May this year, Professor Adalbert Van Brennen, seventy, who worked at the Suggestive Psychotherapy Clinic, was found dead in his bed. There was no sign of a struggle or blows, no evidence of a break-in via the windows of his room or the front door of the house. It appears that he died in his sleep. Then New York: on 16 July, Dr William Stanhope was found dead in the early morning. He was forty-three and worked at the Neurology Institute and, like Professor Van Brennen, despite his closed eyes, he looked … well, I'll let you guess!'

'Absolutely terrified!' Fourier was the first to cry.

'Exactly. In both cases, despite the very strange circumstances, the cause of death was recorded as bleeding in the brain, although the symptoms did not corroborate the theory.'

'There was no autopsy?'

'It was not considered necessary.'

'Did the articles say what they were working on?' I asked.

'The Neurology Institute in New York is known for its interest in nervous disorders and behavioural disorders in the young. But Dr Stanhope seems to have specialised in sleep-related illnesses. As for Professor Van Brennen, he treated certain psychological imbalances through hypnosis. He began his career at the Salpêtrière hospital under Charcot at the end of the 1880s.'

'So both men were carrying out research into sleep and dreams,' I observed.

'By digging a bit, I found another mention of this Van Brennen. There was a paper on his Suggestive Psychotherapy Clinic in a scientific magazine a few months before his death. The clinic clearly treated some rather loopy cases. Among other things, Professor Van Brennen had apparently treated a patient suffering from *Hyperesthesia psychosexualis* for a long time.'

'What?' said Fourier.

'Psychosexual hyperesthesia. His patient was convinced that he was the victim of a lascivious creature who tormented him every night.'

'Ah, yes! Those ethereal spirits our dear Marquis was so fond of!'

'Van Brennen was convinced that he could be treated with hypnosis.'

'And did it work?'

'The article didn't say.'

In the space of an instant, images from my dream came back to me. I saw the face of the unknown woman bent over mine and experienced again the taste of her sweet hair between my lips and the mellow heat of her skin. I chased away the vision with a reflex movement of my hand.

'No other cases of Deadly Sleep?' asked James.

'I went as far back as the summer of 1932 but I couldn't find anything else. No, the whole thing definitely seems to have started with the death of Professor Van Brennen on 9 May this year.'

'Of course,' my friend speculated out loud, 'if we could find out whether a chap who looked vaguely like a mad doctor had tried to meet the two victims a few days before their deaths, it would certainly make our case easier.'

'How can we find out?'

'Maybe the Sûreté could contact the relevant police forces?'

'That might take time but you're right, we must try everything. I will give orders to that effect. Lacroix, my congratulations! That was good work.'

'So from now on we must consider that five deaths have occurred in similar circumstances,' I declared. 'Adalbert Van Brennen on 9 May; Percival Crowles on 5 June; William Stanhope on 16 July; Pierre Ducros on 26 August; and finally the Marquis de Brindillac last week on 13 October.'

James shivered. 'Five deaths in the course of six months, that's a lot.'

'Too many. Time is short,' confirmed Fourier. 'I think that a meeting with the leader of the Surrealist group is called for.'

'Yes. We have to find out why our Austrian chap seems to be so interested in him or one of his friends, and if he has already tried to contact them.'

'There again I can help, Superintendent,' said Lacroix. 'André is extremely hostile towards anyone who even remotely resembles a police officer. With all due respect, you will have more chance of obtaining information if I accompany you.'

'Fine! I accept your proposal, Lacroix. The best thing would be to go to his home immediately – if you see no objection of course.'

'None.'

'In the meantime, James, shall we go and see those nice people at the Institut Métapsychique? Perhaps they will remember Hans-Rudolf von Öberlin's visit. And they can tell us about the lecture the Marquis de Brindillac planned to give. I am very curious to know what it was going to be about.'

'An excellent idea, gentlemen! Then it will be time to go to the Café de la Place Blanche. Hopefully our man will appear. But this time, dash it all, I won't let him get away!'

It was settled. Midday sounded at the church of Saint-Merri. We agreed to meet at Place Blanche at six o'clock sharp.

'It wouldn't be a good idea to be seen together at the Surrealists' café,' added Fourier, rising. 'Is there somewhere else we could meet?'

'The Cyrano brasserie,' replied Lacroix. 'It's their old headquarters and it's very near, on the other side of the square.'

'Perfect. Let's meet there, gentlemen. Are you coming, Lacroix?'

'Why did they change their headquarters?' I asked.

'The owner didn't care for broken tables …'

The hotel doors closed behind the superintendent and Lacroix, and we watched them through the window as they made their way down Rue des Lombards.

'Speaking of tables,' cried James, 'I've just realised that I haven't eaten a thing! Let's go and have a good meal.'

X

A VISIT TO THE INSTITUT MÉTAPSYCHIQUE

When the taxi dropped us at No. 89 Avenue Niel, a hundred yards away from Place Pereire, I admired the façade of the famous house for a few seconds.

Nestling between two much taller buildings, it was two storeys high (not counting the attic under the mansard roof which had been converted into flats in the traditional Haussmann style) and was less imposing than I had imagined. But it had an indefinable charm, largely due to the reputation for brimstone and mystery the Institut had acquired after fifteen years of research on the very margins of science.

It was here that Arthur Conan Doyle had set a chapter of his novel *The Land of Mist* in 1926 although, for reasons which escaped me, he had located the metapsychists' headquarters in Avenue de Wagram instead of Avenue Niel. It was here too that Malone, Mailey and Roxton, Professor Challenger's friends, had witnessed materialisation experiments which had left them flabbergasted.

The most renowned mediums had crossed the threshold of this building and been put under the microscope by the Institut's team of researchers. Eva C. went through just such an ordeal. Jean Guzik held nearly eighty séances during which he revealed his terrible ghosts of animals, eagles, dogs and rodents, and the enormous beast, a kind of bear or Pithecanthropus, which had so frightened those present. Luwig Kahn, the man who could read without using his eyes, was extensively studied. Franek Kluski submitted to dozens of meetings where he demonstrated his gift for making ghosts materialise and allowed casts to be made of spirit hands. Pascal Forthuny, the great clairvoyant, displayed the full measure of his talent. A few months earlier the Austrian, Rudi Schneider, had been subjected to relentless testing.

'I hope there's someone there,' I remarked, approaching the front door.

'Bah! There should be an ectoplasm to open the door at least.'

I only had to knock once before a uniformed butler opened the door.

'Messieurs, are you here for the meeting?'

'Uh, not exactly. We're detectives. This is my associate, James Trelawney. My name is Andrew Fowler Singleton. We would like to talk to Professor Richet.'

'Unfortunately, the professor has been detained elsewhere. He will not be here today.'

'Perhaps Dr Osty could see us then?'

'I'm afraid that won't be possible either. A séance is to be held shortly in the assembly room. Dr Osty is on the second floor at the moment, having tea with our medium. He is helping him relax and prepare for the séance properly.'

'Oh, what a pity!'

As far as we could judge through the half-open door, the hall was filled with people. Behind the butler we could see small groups of men and women chatting.

'Edgar, why are these gentlemen not coming in?' said a voice suddenly. We only saw the man's face a few moments later.

He was about fifty, tall, with carefully brushed grey hair and a slightly aristocratic and mannered air.

'These gentlemen are detectives. They would like to see Dr Osty.'

'How do you do. Detectives you say?'

'Mr Trelawney and Mr Singleton.'

'Trelawney? Singleton? That's strange, I've heard your names somewhere before. Yes, of course! What was I thinking? Your reputation has been much discussed in the spiritualist press. Please, come in. I am honoured to meet you.'

We entered the hall where approximately thirty people were standing around in five or six groups. They could not be all the guests though because two other groups were going up the large staircase opposite us, passing a footman coming downstairs with a tray.

'Allow me to introduce myself. Paul de Vallemont. I am a friend of Dr Osty and Professor Richet's, and incidentally one of the vice-presidents of the Institut. The professor is detained in Switzerland for a few days. As Edgar told you, Dr Osty is going to introduce someone who promises to be the king of clairvoyants, maybe even more talented than dear Forthuny. So I fear that you will be disappointed.'

'Is that why there are so many people?' asked James, looking around the hall.

'Yes. A few honorary members of the Institut are here, as well as some professors from the Sorbonne and the Académie who accepted our invitation, and not forgetting the great many people who saw the announcement in the *Revue Métapsychique*.'

'Perhaps you can help us, Monsieur de Vallemont,' I said, returning to the reason for our visit.

'I would be delighted, gentlemen. But please, let me offer you a drink!'

The footman was heading towards us and we each took the glass he proffered.

'Canard-Duchêne from 1927. I am told that it is excellent. It is the château of one of our benevolent donors. Ah, I am always very honoured to receive within these walls some of our English sympathisers. You know, we have several of your compatriots on our committee.'

'Actually, I'm American!' my friend corrected him. 'Originally from Boston.'

'And I'm Canadian. From Halifax, Nova Scotia. But that's not important. We should explain that we're investigating—'

'Canadian, but of course! Everyone here has heard of your father and what he has done for the spiritualist movement in your province.'

Once he had started talking, Monsieur de Vallemont was like a runaway train.

'Monsieur de Vallemont,' I resumed, 'we are investigating the death of the Marquis de Brindillac.'

'Oh, the poor Marquis! It is never pleasant to die but what happened in his case was appalling.'

'Did you know him well?'

'Certainly, as did everyone at the Institut Métapsychique. He no longer came to see us very often at Avenue Niel but I visited him at his château in Étampes on two or three occasions.'

'Have you been there recently?' asked James.

'The last time was in June. Dr Osty went there four or five weeks before his death.'

'That is just why we would like to see him. The Marquis de Brindillac was working on sleep and dreams – is that correct?'

'Indeed. It is a fascinating subject, it is true. The Marquis asserted that it was new psychic territory to be explored, and is almost entirely untouched at present. Do you realise that at a time of the general theory of relativity and quantum mechanics, we still don't know anything about sleep? And yet we devote nearly a third of our lives to it. As for dreams, our ignorance is even more striking.

Come, could you tell me what dreams are for?'

'To provide a few pleasant moments of relaxation,' replied James. 'Sort of cheap holidays where the brain distracts us by sailing along through a wonderland.'

'You may be right, Monsieur Trelawney. But, in fact, no one really knows what to make of them. It is one of the greatest mysteries the human mind has ever had to solve. And that is exactly what our dear departed friend was working on. He spent entire nights, poor man, in the work room of his château watching over the rest of his household who served as case studies.'

'To what purpose?'

'Understanding when dreams appear. He discovered that they actually occupy a fairly small proportion of the time devoted to sleep. They appear one and a half hours after we fall asleep and return regularly in brief sequences of about twenty minutes. But for most of the night our bodies and minds are completely inert.'

'He was also studying lucid dreams, I believe.'

'You are right, Monsieur Singleton. He was both fascinated and disturbed by his ability to control his dreams and to pace around inside them like an actor on stage. Have you ever experienced a lucid dream?'

'Never!' replied James. 'And I must admit that I very rarely remember my dreams. Even the most banal ones.'

I had no desire to talk about my recent personal experience in the matter so I avoided answering by asking another question.

'We understand that the Institut Métapsychique had been planning a public lecture on the Marquis's work at the beginning of next year. Do you know the details?'

'I'm afraid not. Actually, I think that Dr Osty would find it very difficult to tell you as well.'

'Wasn't he arranging the meeting in consultation with Auguste de Brindillac?'

'I think it was more that the Marquis had managed to convince him of the importance of such a meeting, while remaining as evasive as possible about what he was actually going to say. The Marquis was like a child. He loved surprising the world and creating an event. Dr Osty had sufficient confidence in the old professor's intelligence and wisdom to agree at once to organise the lecture.'

'So no one knew exactly what the Marquis wanted to say on that day?'

'No one.'

'Not even an inkling?'

'I can only repeat what the Marquis told Dr Osty: a new world is opening up before us. It's not terribly enlightening, is it? We will know more when Amélie de Brindillac has finished deciphering her father's work and we publish it.'

'One more question, Monsieur de Vallemont. Someone came to the Institut Métapsychique about ten days ago. More precisely, between Tuesday 9 and Saturday 13 October. He is an Austrian who claims to be a professor in Vienna.'

'Many people come here, from all over Europe. We are a very active society.'

'He probably introduced himself as Hans-Rudolf von Öberlin ...'

'Sorry, but I have no memory for names.'

'According to our information, he would be about sixty-five, with long white hair and enormous sideburns, a hooked nose and, above all, very dark, calculating eyes which make an impression on everyone—'

'Oh, those eyes! Of course I remember! How could I forget? The man did indeed come here. It was, let's see ... Wednesday 10 October, mid-afternoon.'

'So you saw him?'

'I did more than that. I was the one who received him.'

'Monsieur de Vallemont!' cried James. 'Let Dr Osty prepare for his meeting. You are the man we need!'

At the top of the staircase the footman rang a small bell to rally the troops. The guests waiting in the hall hurried up the stairs.

'Gentlemen, I hope you will do us the honour of attending the meeting? It promises to be fascinating. If you wait until the end, Dr Osty will be happy to speak to you.'

James and I exchanged a look. We had several questions to ask Monsieur de Vallemont but he clearly didn't want to miss the start of the festivities for anything.

'With pleasure,' I replied, 'if you will allow me to discuss a few small details with you on the way to the assembly room.'

'Of course. Follow me, gentlemen, follow me,' he said, leading us towards the carpeted stairs. 'Oh! Since you are connoisseurs, did you know that our laboratory for elemental chemistry is behind that door over there? A beautiful room measuring thirty foot by fifteen, with all the necessary recording equipment – both photographic and sound – phosphorus lamps, infrared transmitters, luminescent screens made of zinc sulphide, etc. In this laboratory we can carry out the most complicated experiments on fluidic materialisations or telepathic phenomena. It is one of our pride and joys at the Institut. If you wish, I can show you round.'

'With pleasure … another time!' replied my associate. 'Monsieur de Vallemont, what did this fellow want to know?'

'The same as you.'

'Meaning?'

'What the Marquis was working on.'

'Did you tell him?'

'I only told him what I knew. There was no reason to make a secret of it.'

'And that's all?'

'In the end, he proved to be a bit too insistent. I explained that if he wanted to know more he'd have to wait until the start of next year, when it was anticipated that the Marquis would present the results of his research in public. The news seemed to disturb him.'

'Did he tell you his profession?'

'A doctor in experimental psychology. It was apparently in that capacity that he wanted to know about the work of Auguste de Brindillac. I remarked that the best thing, then, was to speak to Brindillac himself. He retorted that he intended to. Then he shook my hand and left, smiling unpleasantly.'

'Nothing more?'

'No.'

'Had you seen him before?'

'Never.'

'You hadn't come across him anywhere at all?'

'I would have remembered. He had a strange way of staring at you as if he wanted to examine the very depths of your thoughts. Something like that isn't easily forgotten. But I am wondering why he interests you. Have you established a connection between him and the death of the Marquis de Brindillac?'

'No. We're simply gathering information.'

We had reached the top of the staircase. Paul de Vallemont was hurrying to reach the assembly room as quickly as possible.

'Monsieur,' I resumed, trying to detain him a little longer as we approached the door. 'Have you read the article in *Paris-Soir* about the death of a poet in similar circumstances to Auguste de Brindillac?'

'Of course. Like the rest of Paris, I imagine.'

'What did you think?'

'That it is an extraordinary way to die ... So twice in the space of a few weeks is very strange.'

'Precisely. You are used to dealing with the unusual, the bizarre and the extraordinary here. You must have an opinion.'

Paul de Vallemont turned his head towards the assembly-room door regretfully. We heard the sound of a male voice. The meeting had begun. Politeness prevented our host from ending the conversation too abruptly but we knew that we only had a few more seconds.

'Yes, we deal with the extraordinary every single day,' he said as courteously as ever. 'Look, behind the other door over there, on the other side of the landing, is our library; it is one of the largest collections in the world relating to the other side and the supernatural. What were we talking about? Oh yes, the article! My colleagues and I have discussed it at length, as vigorously as we discussed the death of the poor Marquis at the beginning of the week. A Management and Administration Committee meeting was also organised yesterday morning to examine the issue.'

While speaking, Paul de Vallemont had edged towards the doorway and we followed him into the Institut's vast assembly room, reserved for official receptions and conferences. Inside, nearly a hundred and fifty people were sitting on either side of a central aisle. They were listening with rapt attention to a man dressed entirely in black whom I took to be Dr Osty. He was on a kind of stage at the end of the room and had already begun introducing the guest next to him. The latter (apparently the medium) was a small man with a pale face who was outwardly respectable-looking. Sitting on a chair, while Dr Osty was standing, the clairvoyant was examining the audience, visibly impressed.

We had to wrap up the conversation quickly before Monsieur de Vallemont left us entirely.

'What conclusion did you come to at your committee meeting?' I asked in a low voice.

'As often happens at the Institut, opinions were divided into two camps. According to the first, that of the scientists, the Marquis de Brindillac and the poet Pierre Ducros were prey to a hallucination.'

'What do you mean?'

'Our colleague, the venerable Antoine de Méricourt, a professor at the Collège de France, quoted the work of a certain Dr Schatzman[13] in support of this theory. Schatzman discusses different kinds of hallucinations, particularly nocturnal illusions. Using this research, and other studies to back up his view, Méricourt claims that it is possible for a sleeper to awake suddenly during the night in a state of languor, paralysed, and be the victim, through an uncontrollable surge in cerebral activity, of a series of visual and aural hallucinations which may cause a panicky fear in him.'[14]

'And is it possible to die from that?'

'I don't … Possibly … Probably … An ad hoc committee was created to look into it but it will not present its conclusions for several weeks. Now, gentlemen, I must leave you. As vice-chairman, I must be in the front row. I look forward to seeing you after the meeting … or on another occasion soon.'

'Monsieur de Vallemont,' I pleaded, touching his sleeve, 'you haven't told us what the other group thought.'

'Oh, excuse me! Well, according to the spiritualist camp, the guilty parties should be sought among the Invisible.'

'The Invisible?'

'Yes. The Ancients, from whom we have so much to learn, considered dreams to be privileged access to the world of spirits. They had an expression for it: the gates of sleep. Never forget, gentlemen, that the world on to which these gates open is full of formidable shades, bloodthirsty grubs and diabolical lemures. Some of these creatures found a way to besiege the psyche of the Marquis and the poet, and plagued them until death followed. If that theory is true, what an ordeal their last night must have been!'

This time Paul de Vallemont didn't give us time to reply. He inclined his head quickly and then walked down the central aisle and slid discreetly into an empty chair just in front of the platform.

'Whatever the correct theory,' exclaimed James after a few moments' silence, sounding both alarmed and disappointed, 'if these people are right, we'll be unemployed, my friend! No more mystery to get our teeth into! And our Austrian cleared of all suspicion! It's puzzling to say the least!'

I admit that I no longer knew what to think myself. I was also starting to feel my lack of sleep cruelly and was suddenly overwhelmed with weariness. I suggested that we sit down and listen to the meeting for a while.

On stage Dr Osty had stopped talking in order to let the medium concentrate. Sitting back in his chair with his eyes closed, he had gone into a trance. There was a noticeable change in his breathing, his eyelids quivered and his hands trembled slightly on his knees. We heard a kind of panting which sounded like a small animal. Then the noise grew fainter before stopping completely. The man began to breathe normally. After a minute, he opened his eyes. In a thin voice he said, 'I am here. The séance may begin.'

Dr Osty turned to the audience.

'Ladies and gentlemen, Monsieur Pfizer is now in a light state of hypnosis. Outwardly, there is nothing to see. His mind is as active as when he is awake but, in reality, Monsieur Pfizer now possesses far greater powers of acquiring knowledge than usual. If he is spoken to, he can hold a conversation without difficulty, whatever the subject. At the same time, he is capable of gleaning a fragmented knowledge of very intimate events concerning his interlocutor, knowledge which in normal conditions it would be impossible for Mr Pfizer to obtain through the usual sensory channels.

'As you will soon realise, Monsieur Pfizer's visions are initially mainly symbolic. He doesn't perceive the truth clearly and precisely like reading a book or looking at a photograph. No, if he makes a connection with someone from the audience, a flow of mental images suddenly appears in his consciousness and he becomes aware of vague impressions, colours, isolated words, even memories from his own past which run on one after the other like a rebus that he must then decipher.

'Ladies and gentlemen, you who are seated in this room and do us the honour of participating in this new experiment, I suggest that we begin the séance. Monsieur Pfizer and I will wander among you. Monsieur Pfizer, please rise and follow me! Monsieur Pfizer is going to try to *see* you.'

The two men left the platform and began their circuit of the room. Dr Osty walked next to the medium who, apart from a rather fixed expression, displayed none of the strange behaviour one might have expected from someone in a state of hypnosis or a trance.

Pfizer stopped in front of a large lady sitting next to the central aisle, dressed in a woollen jacket and a black crepe hat. He closed his eyes and appeared to sink into a state of artificial sleep again but this time it was lighter and did not last as long. Then he opened his eyes and spoke to her.

'Madame, I suddenly have a feeling of suffocation. It is hot, very hot, as if the temperature in the room has increased greatly. I feel breathless; I almost feel nauseous. I can make out several figures embracing. They look similar, perhaps they are related. I think that it is a gathering of some kind, a reunion. It is still very hot. Do you or someone close to you have an estranged sibling?'

'Wait a moment,' the medium continued, without giving the woman time to reply. 'It's not a reunion but the island of Réunion! Do you know someone from the island of Réunion, Madame? Or someone who is coming back from there?'

113

'My son!' exclaimed the large lady.

'Is he returning because he is ill?'

'Yes.'

'Is it his heart?'

'Yes, his heart! He suffers from cardiac insufficiency. He had to come back immediately. He was in charge of a trading post.'

Monsieur Pfizer bowed to the lady, satisfied, and moved away, accompanied by Dr Osty.

'What is this circus act?' asked my friend, attracting the ire of our neighbours. 'That lady is obviously in league with the medium.'

Although our shared experience had taught us always to keep an open mind when faced with the fantastic and the supernatural, we also knew very well that psychic research regularly came up against deception and falsification. Since the case of the Empty Circle, during which we had encountered the sadly infamous Sprengler, a sham expert on thought transmission who was able to guess what was in the pockets of members of the audience apparently chosen at random, my colleague was very sceptical of all supposed clairvoyant mediums.

Voices murmured 'Shh!' and 'Quiet!' all around us.

As for the medium, he wandered about for a few minutes before stopping in front of a row and meeting the gaze of a severe-looking man.

'That's strange, I can hear birdsong. Is your name Bird?'

'No, my name is Sparrow!'

There was loud laughter from the audience and the gentleman seemed very annoyed.

'Preposterous!' commented my friend sombrely.

'Shh! Shh!'

Pfizer and Dr Osty began walking again.

This time the clairvoyant was drawn to a young blonde woman.

She seemed very anxious and resisted slightly when Pfizer leant towards her to take her handbag. The medium reassured her with a few well-chosen words and held the bag for several moments, his eyes closed. Then he put it down and began to comment on the visions which were invading his consciousness.

'This will seem ridiculous to you but I have the feeling that this handbag is suffering. It is unwell. I feel pain in it. Ah! Another thing, I hear a name. Octave. Does the name Octave mean anything to you, Mademoiselle?'

'That is my fiancé's name,' replied the young woman, confused.

'Does he work with leather? Or in the clothing industry?'

'No, he's an engineer.'

'I don't understand.'

The medium opened his eyes.

'The pain is increasing and the bag is changing colour. It's not brown any more, it's white, white as a sheet. It is afraid, it's hiding. Is Octave suffering?'

'He is very ill.'

'It's strange, I see myself as a child playing near the marshes of Saint-Gond. My mother is telling me, "You must not put water from the marshes in your mouth, it's dirty." Does Octave work in the marshes?'

'Yes, he has returned from south-west Baghdad.'

'Leather! Skin! Octave has caught a skin disease!'

'He is suffering from very serious lupus,' said the young lady with tears in her eyes. 'His doctor has put him in quarantine. He fears that there is no cure and that he caught it during work to drain the peat bogs.'

'Ah! I have an image of a woman in a black apron who keeps gesturing. She is scrubbing, she is scouring, she is polishing, she doesn't stop for a moment. Wait, there is a word: "ménage". It is coming through loud and clear. Does it mean anything to you? Ménage?'

'Ménage? Ménage! Goodness me, no. Oh yes, possibly! I think that Ménage was the maiden name of Octave's mother. Jeanne Ménage. She died two years ago.'

'Wait a moment! The woman in the black apron has become a child and she too is polishing a handbag. Did Octave's mother suffer from a skin disease?'

'Not that I know of.'

'The child is rubbing the bag more vigorously and the leather is losing its colour. Mademoiselle, your fiancé is not suffering from lupus. The marshes have nothing to do with it. It is a severe form of eczema, a hereditary form. His mother had it when she was little. There is no danger, I assure you, my child.'

The young woman could not hold back her tears. The medium shook her warmly by the hand and then moved away, deeply affected himself, wishing her well.

The room, which had remained quiet until then, began to hum with muffled comments and exclamations. A few people started to applaud but Dr Osty raised his hand for silence.

I felt James seething next to me.

'Let's go,' he said.

'Very well.'

Pfizer and Osty had reached the back of the room. The medium stopped three rows in front of us. It would have been rude to leave the meeting just then.

Although I did not share James's suspicion, I was finding it difficult to form a definite opinion about what we were witnessing. I knew the reputation of the Institut Métapsychique and Dr Osty was highly regarded. But might this good doctor himself be the dupe of a malicious charlatan?

'Let's wait until he goes to the other side of the aisle,' I whispered. 'Then we can leave.'

I assumed that the medium was going to address someone in front of him but he unexpectedly turned to me. I was sitting in the back row outside his field of vision. As soon as his gaze fell on me I became extremely anxious that my most private thoughts, my most secret desires, might be revealed. Monsieur Pfizer's clairvoyance was suddenly very disturbing.

He approached me calmly, closed his eyes and almost immediately opened them again.

'I hear a distant voice from a place which doesn't seem to be of this world. The face is that of a young, extraordinarily beautiful blonde woman. She is calling you. It is a spirit. No, I don't feel that she is dead. Who is she? Have you ever heard her voice?'

'No,' I replied uncertainly.

'She is afraid for you.'

'I don't know what you're talking about.'

I was not telling the truth, obviously. I was convinced that he was talking about my stranger from the steamer. But how was that possible since all that was only dreams and illusions? Mere figments of the imagination!

'You surprise me greatly, Monsieur. This voice is very insistent. She is asking you to believe in her. She repeats it most emphatically. Now I see something else. It is a vast landscape. A valley, a wide green valley, and a fast-flowing river running through it. I see paddle steamers and a castle sitting high above, with a pointed roof on one of its towers.'

There was no doubt about it. His vision was the landscape of *fata Morgana* which had appeared in the Channel between Dover and Calais. What was I to make of it?

'The young lady is even further away. I can hear her saying

something. It's not very clear. "Good night Vienna!" Yes, I think that's it: "Good night Vienna!" Her voice is fading. She's disappearing into the night. Does that mean anything to you?'

'Good night Vienna,' I repeated, increasingly rattled. 'No, it doesn't mean anything to me.'

'There is also a train. It is travelling fast. Do you see a connection?'

'A train? For Paris? London?'

'No, it's heading east. A train you must not miss. Now I can hear the ticking of a clock. Wait! It's striking. It's evening. Hold on, I can hear eight strokes. But the face is only showing seven minutes to eight. That's strange. The mechanism must be broken. Seven minutes to eight! Does that time mean anything?'

'No,' I replied.

'Truly nothing?'

'Nothing at all.'

'I'm sorry, Monsieur. It's gone. The images have disappeared. For good.'

The medium bowed to me politely and moved away with the director of the Institut towards other members of the audience, but I was not paying attention any more. I sat dumbfounded on my seat, lost in interminable arguments and objections.

Pfizer had been spot on in describing the magical valley from the mirage and referring to a young blonde woman in my immediate psychic environment. Did he really have a gift for clairvoyance? What about his other allusions (the east, the train and so on) and what connection did it have with the Deadly Sleep case? Was there a hidden meaning? And if so, why didn't I understand it?

On the other hand, his reference to a blonde woman was very vague. I was probably attributing it to my stranger from the steamer without grounds. My dreams from the last few nights kept following me. Sham mediums, although they were fakes, were always excellent observers. Had Pfizer been able to pick up certain clues from my behaviour?

As I succumbed to a combination of shock and fatigue, my face must have turned alarmingly pale because James took me by the arm and forced me to stand up. Barely aware of what was happening around me, I obediently followed him out of the Institut's great assembly room to the deserted pavement of Avenue Niel.

The fresh air revived me.

XI

AT THE CAFÉ DE LA PLACE BLANCHE

'He's a pain in the neck, that Monsieur Breton!' the superintendent fulminated as he and Lacroix sat down at our table at the Cyrano.

For the last three-quarters of an hour we had been sitting in the sunshine outside the brasserie and the area's lively atmosphere had quite restored me. The mood was carefree and light-hearted. Everything around us seemed to suggest frivolous dreams, the pleasure of the senses and a complete disregard for time passing.

Just to our right was the city's most flamboyant music hall, the Moulin Rouge, where the whole world came to dance to the rhythm of quadrilles, waltzes and polkas. It was almost aperitif time. On the other side of the square, on the corner of Rue Blanche and Rue Fontaine, the tables outside the café which served as the Surrealists' headquarters were beginning to fill up with students and artists. Behind us, a constant stream of apprentice seamstresses and dressmakers were leaving the workshops of Montmartre. To our left, further away on Boulevard de Clichy, behind the Art Nouveau métro station, if you craned your neck you could just see the heavy sculpted doors of the cabarets of Le Ciel and L'Enfer. There, for less than a couple of francs, visitors could choose between heavenly bliss and the torments of hell; either way, it came with smiling girls and strong liquor. Further away still, beyond Pigalle, was the Medrano circus with its jugglers and female fakirs.

On Place Blanche the chaotic procession of cars, bicycles and omnibuses was never-ending, accompanied by the sound of horns, hooters and klaxons. We were in the very heart of gay Paree. In a few hours, when the sun went down, it would be in full swing.

After leaving the Institut, James and I had gone for a gentle amble along Avenue de Villiers and Boulevard des Batignolles up to Place de Clichy. To kill time, I had bought a second copy of *Nadja* and a copy of *Les Vases communicants* published by Éditions des Cahiers Libres in 1932. After enquiring at the bookshop about Monsieur Breton's latest work, I had also bought the *Point du jour* collection which had been published at the beginning of summer in *La Nouvelle Revue française*.

When Fourier and Lacroix arrived, I was absorbed in the opening pages of *Nadja*. As for James, he had not yet wearied of the city's spectacle.

'Yes, indeed! An utter pain in the neck!' the superintendent repeated, ordering a glass of wine. 'He kept us hanging about for ages before throwing us out on our ear, you might say!'

'What do you mean, Superintendent?' asked my friend, trying not to laugh. 'Were you not able to question him?'

'Oh yes! But it wasn't much help. He was very uncooperative and gave us a whole lot of rubbish about the philosophical inanity of sleuths like Sherlock Holmes and Dupin. Finally, Monsieur deigned to reply that he had not noticed anything unusual. No so-called Austrians fitting the description we had given him have tried to contact him.'

'So not much use then.'

'No, and worse still, after letting slip that my men and I would be present this evening at the Café de la Place Blanche, he became furious and threatened to kick up a fuss if he saw any of our "henchmen" at his next meeting.'

'It doesn't really matter since we decided that Lacroix would take care of it.'

'Breton was certainly livid,' replied the journalist. 'After seeing me with a superintendent from the Sûreté, I'm not sure that my presence will be acceptable to him either. And it would appear that he has still not got over one of my criticisms of the Second Manifesto published in *Paris-Soir* nearly ... oh, four years ago. If Breton threatens to make a scene, take my word for it that he will not hesitate to do so in spectacular style. We can't take that risk.'

'No, we mustn't take any risks,' added Fourier. 'If Monsieur Breton doesn't want us in the Café de la Place Blanche, very well then, we won't be there!'

'What?' I exclaimed. 'You can't just give up!'

'Of course not! But I thought that you and James could go instead. I'll stay outside with my men. All we need is for our suspect to turn up this evening. He leaves the brasserie and gotcha! We pounce. Lacroix can identify him once we've nabbed him.'

'Couldn't we arrest him before he goes into the café?' suggested James.

'Too risky. I want us to have time to watch him. We mustn't make any mistakes. Let me remind you that this is our only chance to grab him.'

'Very well. So how do we proceed?'

'Once you've spotted him, study his behaviour. When it looks as if he's about to leave, one of you – let's say you, Singleton – will go out ahead of him and light a cigarette on the pavement. That will be the signal. I will be nearby with my men. They are already in place around the café as we speak – praying that our suspect comes back!'

'Ah!' cried James, draining his glass of Dubonnet. 'That's better. What time is it?'

'Twenty past six,' replied Lacroix. 'I think you'd better be off. Breton will be there soon, if he hasn't arrived already. He lives nearby at 42 Rue Fontaine.'

'What does this Breton fellow look like?'

'I think,' I said, flicking through my copy of *Nadja*, 'that there is a photo of him at the back of the book. Yes, look!'

'He hasn't changed,' added Lacroix. 'You'll recognise him immediately.'

James and I paid for our drinks and crossed the square, heading for the Surrealists' brasserie. It had been agreed that Lacroix and Fourier would take up their positions in a few minutes, Lacroix by the métro station and Fourier at the corner of Rue Fontaine and Boulevard de Clichy.

According to Lacroix, the meeting was always held indoors whatever the weather, next to the wooden staircase.

As soon as we entered the café we recognised Breton. He was sitting in the left-hand corner of the room, at the centre of a large table surrounded by empty seats, dressed in a green velvet jacket – as green as the drink in front of him – and a tie with red spots. He was reading a newspaper and making disparaging comments about the author of the article. Next to him on the imitation-leather bench was a pretty young woman with a sweet, expressive face. A pale blonde, she was sipping a glass of flavoured milk and her eyes were lovingly fixed on the leader of the Surrealists. This was Jacqueline Lamba (as I discovered later), a 24-year-old painter with whom Breton was madly in love. They had married a few weeks earlier.

We took a table near the window looking on to Rue Blanche from where we could see Dupuytren's heavy frame leaning against a lamppost. There was no sign of Fourier though; he was taking care to stay out of sight.

From our position we could observe the meeting at leisure when it began, as well as the other tables in the room. For a change, we ordered two glasses of an aniseed aperitif from the waiter.

Our corner was relatively quiet. By straining our ears we could make out what the newlyweds were saying. In response to an acid remark from Breton on an aspect of the Doumergue cabinet, I heard his companion advise him, with a tender smile, not to spend his nights writing until dawn any more.

'Really, my darling, lack of sleep doesn't agree with you,' she said, stroking his hand.

André and Jacqueline were not alone for long. A few minutes later two men and a woman appeared. One of the newcomers was tall and thin with short blond hair and an asymmetrical face (his photograph was in my copy of *Nadja*; his name was Paul Éluard). The other one was just as thin, had brown hair and very pale skin, and looked like a Sicilian shepherd. The young woman had long black hair worn in a bun. She appeared to be with Éluard.

Before long there were half a dozen people around the table. The waiter immediately brought the new arrivals drinks, generally spirits – lemon Picon, Mandarin-curaçao, Ricard – and the conversation flowed easily. Breton, his long hair pulled back, his blue eyes ringed with dark shadows, dominated this inner circle with an air of natural authority, his head wreathed in thick cigarette smoke. As the others talked, he would throw in the occasional comment, which was rarely challenged.

'Do you realise, James, that those are some of the most brilliant writers of our dreary age? Monsieur Breton, for example, has one of the most penetrating minds I have ever read. Only in Paris can you come across such dazzling brilliance.'

'Astonishing!' said my friend, his eyes scanning the room. 'You should be looking to see if our fellow is here, rather than going into literary raptures.'

'He doesn't appear to be so far.'

The surrounding tables were now occupied by infatuated young couples, men in tweed suits quietly reading the paper and boisterous young people trying to get the Surrealists to notice them. At the other end of the room a man with his hair cut in a bob, a very long goatee and small blue glasses was examining some sheet music.

No trace of our quarry and, except for the table of students, none of the customers appeared to be paying any attention to the Surrealist meeting.

Among the Surrealists, a second and then a third round of drinks had raised spirits and a glorious cacophony could now be heard. The booming voices of the most voluble were punctuated by the clinking of glasses, the scraping of chairs and bursts of laughter.

'Listen to them,' said my friend, indicating the group where Breton had just caused hilarity. 'I get the feeling he's telling them about the misfortunes of Fourier and Lacroix this afternoon.'

At the same time Breton half rose from his chair, his chest puffed out like a hussar's, and cast a blazing eye around the room, ready to run through with his imaginary lance any superintendent, Surrealist dissenter or hypothetical officer from the Sûreté who dared to show his face.

The group was quiet while the inspection took place. Suddenly, general wild laughter broke out. Breton sat down again and the conversation resumed with even greater intensity.

'Phew!' said James, taking a gulp of his drink. 'For a moment I thought he was going to pounce on us.'

Outside, night had fallen. Dupuytren had swapped his lamppost for another one, a little further down the street.

The meeting continued in the same friendly mood until the end. As the time for dancing and cabarets approached, the newspaper readers were replaced by pretty girls and elegant tourists, fussed over by the multilingual waiters. The students, fed up with being ignored by their elders, had packed up and gone. Only the musician continued to read his notes.

125

'What if it's him?' I murmured, in case the man was watching us from behind his coloured lenses. 'His hair and his beard might be false. And why does he always keep his glasses on?'

'Because otherwise he wouldn't be able to see anything. For goodness' sake! We've been languishing here for over an hour, Andrew. Our Austrian friend clearly didn't feel like going out this evening.'

At around half past seven, the first to leave the Surrealists' table was a man with large ears and a moon face. He was soon followed by a shiny-haired young dandy clinging on to a redhead in a fur-lined cape as though afraid he might lose her.

One after the other the guests departed, warmly bidding farewell to Breton and his muse until they were left alone. That didn't seem to trouble the young woman who put her head lovingly on the poet's shoulder.

They sat in silence for a while, lost in thought, without concerning themselves in the least about the diners who were taking their seats around them.

Finally, they, too, decided to leave. Breton threw a few coins down in front of him and made towards the door. In the middle of the room, halfway between our table and the musician's, he promised his companion in a loud, theatrical voice, as if he wanted the entire brasserie to be his witness, that he would not write that evening and that the night would be hers. She replied with a simple kiss on the hand and led him outside.

'How charming they are, those lovebirds!' said James ironically as we watched them walk off along the pavement.

It was now or never. I leapt from my chair, keeping my eyes on the musician.

'Andrew! What's the matter with you?'

'André Breton wrote in the Second Manifesto that the simplest

Surrealist act was to go into the street, revolver in hand, and start shooting at will,' I recited from memory.

'So what? Do you want to shoot this fellow?' he asked pityingly, glancing at the man. 'You don't even have a gun!'

'No need for a gun. There's a simpler way!'

I strode the short distance over to his table and stopped in front of it.

The man lifted his eyes from his libretto, looking thoroughly perplexed. My tired face, reflected in the blue lenses of his glasses, regained some colour. Suddenly, I tugged sharply on his beard with all my strength.

The loud chatter around me instantly ceased. The waiters' trays froze in midair. The flower seller dropped her bouquets.

A long cry of pain had just rung out around the Café de la Place Blanche.

The beard was real.

XII

LONG LIVE SURREALISM

After being curtly invited to leave the brasserie and never return, James and I decided to call it a night. The superintendent announced that he was returning to Rue des Saussaies to check whether the description given to the Viennese police had yielded any results and whether it was possible to obtain information from his colleagues in Amsterdam and New York on the new cases Lacroix had uncovered. A deadline for the Monday edition obliged Lacroix to return to his typewriter straight away.

Before going our separate ways, we arranged to meet the following day at eleven o'clock at the Hôtel Saint-Merri.

In the meantime James persuaded me to go with him to see Fritz Lang's film *Liliom* at the Electric-Palace, Boulevard des Italiens. At half past eleven, pleading lack of sleep (which was just an excuse as I was in no hurry to go to bed), I returned to the hotel. Although he had hoped for a more exciting end to the evening, James, worried by my pallor, came back with me nonetheless.

Wanting to put off at all costs the moment when I would be at the mercy of my dreams again, I had planned to go to the brasserie in Rue Saint-Martin, which only lowered its shutters very late at night, and peacefully resume reading the books I had bought at Place de Clichy. After a quick wash in my room, I met James at the brasserie. He was dismayed when he saw me taking the André Breton books out of my bag.

'Do you intend to read all night? My word, you'll make yourself ill, Andrew!'

While my friend sipped his cocktail, looking up from the theatre pages of his newspaper from time to time to observe an example of Parisian beauty, I began avidly reading *Les Vases communicants*.

From the very first lines, I found myself in familiar territory. In a review of the current state of research into dreams, André Breton devoted several pages to the famous Hervey de Saint-Denys whose work on lucid dreams Lacroix had praised.

Then came a passage discussing other modern theorists. At the top of the list Breton chose the Viennese doctor Sigmund Freud, author of *The Interpretation of Dreams*, whose method was, in his opinion, by far the 'most original approach'. Throughout the book, André Breton, by seeking to go beyond the eternal opposition of dream and reality, outer and inner worlds, was once more striving to attain what he had described in the Second Manifesto as that 'mental vantage point from which life and death, the real and the imaginary, past and future, communicable and incommunicable, high and low will no longer be seen as contradictions'.

'Fascinating!' I exclaimed, leafing through the final pages. 'Listen to this: "With a little ingenuity it is not impossible to create particular dreams in another person. It would be in no way utopian to claim that, in so doing, one can have a serious impact on their life from a distance."'

'Hmm! What makes me happy is the number of shows on in this city. Andrew, what do you say to seeing a film tomorrow at Gaumont-Palace, Place de Clichy? It has the biggest screen in Europe and seating for six thousand! Or the Parisiana, on Boulevard Poissonnière? Unless you'd prefer a music-hall revue?'

'I thought that since the *époque des sommeils* Breton was less interested in theories of dreamtime activity but that's not the case. The subject still fascinates him just as much.'

'And a drive to Luna-Park from Porte Maillot? They say that the attractions are unique. A funfair – nothing like it for forgetting the problems of an investigation.'

In the face of my indifference, James went back to his newspaper, muttering. I put *Les Vases communicants* on the table and seized *Point du jour*. The book was a collection of sixteen texts, written at different times, the most recent being from about ten months earlier. This last essay, called 'Le Message automatique', reaffirmed the author's interest in the unconscious and the subliminal, in psychic experiments and hallucinations of every kind.

'Reading all this,' I concluded, tapping the last paragraph of 'Le Message automatique' with my finger, 'we must include Breton among the dream specialists. Like Professor Van Brennen, William Stanhope, Percival Crowles, the Marquis de Brindillac and Pierre Ducros, his one-time admirer …'

'What are you getting at?' asked my friend, frowning.

'Nothing. I'm just saying that, like all those eminent researchers, he, too, has applied himself to solving the mysteries of sleep.'

'Must I remind you that the people you've just mentioned all died in the same way? Let's hope that your Breton doesn't end up like them.'

James's words were like a blow to the chest. The mysterious stranger had met Pierre Ducros and, a few days later, the poet had been found dead in his bed. The same man had tried to contact the Marquis de Brindillac and he had been found in the morning, his body stiff and white. Now the Austrian had been seen at the Café de la Place Blanche twice in the last few days. It was probably Breton he was watching and not one of his friends. His interest in him was not in doubt, which meant that the life of the leader of the Surrealists was in danger. It was obvious. It might even be a matter of hours or … minutes.

'James!' I cried. 'Do you remember what Breton's lady friend said to him just before the start of the meeting? She was reproaching him for spending all night writing recently.'

'Yes, I remember perfectly.'

'Well, if he's still alive, it's thanks to those nights he spent awake! However he does it, the Austrian uses his victims' sleep.'

'Some members of the Institut Métapsychique supported the theory of hallucinations. Do you think it's possible to induce such visions? And can they kill?'

'I can't say. In the meantime, the life of André Breton is hanging by a thread. He promised his companion not to stay up tonight …'

That was all it took to galvanise my friend. James threw his newspaper on to the table and rushed out into the street. I just had time to gather my books and shove them in my bag. In less than a minute we had reached Place du Châtelet where a few taxis were waiting.

'Forty-two Rue Fontaine!' I cried to the driver. 'As fast as you can!'

'Right, hold tight!'

The taxi set off at top speed and drove towards Boulevard de Sébastopol. Shortly afterwards, we passed the Gare de l'Est. The driver turned off on to Boulevard de Magenta and put his foot down. He raced along until we reached the elevated railway. There, going through a red light, he turned hard, without slowing down, and continued along Boulevard de Rochechouart. A few moments later we drove past the Café de la Place Blanche which still had its lights on. We turned into Rue Fontaine and drove on a few yards before stopping.

'Here you are, Messieurs! This is 42 Rue Fontaine!' said the driver, pointing to the door of a building near a small theatre with an Art Deco façade.

We paid the fare and got out of the car.

This was a big gamble. After the disappointment of the Café de la Place Blanche earlier, I risked having a strip torn off me by the leader of the Surrealists for disturbing his sleep at two o'clock in the morning. But what did that matter!

'Come on!' I said to my friend. 'There's not a moment to lose.'

The door was closed but James made such a racket, shouting, and kicking and banging the door, that after a few minutes it opened a crack and the sleepy face of an old concierge appeared in the gap.

'Open the door!' James ordered in a tone that brooked no argument. 'Monsieur Breton's flat, where is it? Quickly! It's a matter of life and death!'

'At the end of the corridor,' mumbled the concierge. 'In the courtyard, the building at the back. His studio is on the fourth floor ...'

'Thank you!'

We ran down a long, cold, dark corridor to a second door opening on to a small courtyard. Breton lived in the building behind, the windows of which looked out over Boulevard de Clichy.

We took the squalid stairs two at a time and stopped, out of breath, in front of a door with the number 1713 written in large stylised figures.

'What do those numbers mean?' asked James, putting his ear to the keyhole.

'They're written so that the 1 and the 7 look like a capital A and the 1 and the 3 like a B.'

'A.B.? As in André Breton's initials!'

'We'll think about it later. Can you hear anything?'

'No, nothing.'

'For God's sake!'

'So? Shall we leave it?'

'Out of the question.'

I was preparing to raise my fist when cries could be heard coming from inside the flat.

'André! André!'

I knocked on the door. Inside the cries got louder.

James pushed me to one side. He took a run up and threw himself with all his might against the door. It gave way immediately. The wood splintered around the lock.

'Help! Help!'

The voice came from the back of the studio, which was illuminated by a bare bulb.

We ran towards the light, trying with every step not to tread on the collector's items and South Sea masks which were lying around everywhere. Through the half-open door we could see André Breton lying on the bed in his pyjamas. There was a look of pure terror on his face, as if, beneath his closed lids, the writer's mind was imprisoned in a nightmare from which it was impossible for him to escape. Leaning over him, her cheeks damp with tears, Jacqueline was shaking him violently, saying his name over and over again to make him wake up.

It was not too late; he was still breathing, although with difficulty. His chest jerked nervously. After a few seconds of confusion, we hurried over to him. Seizing him under the arms, we eventually managed to sit him up and lean him against the headboard. We slapped his face and vigorously urged him back to consciousness.

At last Breton opened his eyes. He was completely lost and didn't understand what had happened to him or why there were two strangers in his bedroom. He feverishly sought the face of his companion and, seeing her by his side, his anxiety seemed to fade. Finally, as he became aware of the situation and what he had escaped, he turned to us and gripped our wrists.

'Messieurs! Thanks to you, Surrealism is safe!'

XIII

OBJECTIVE: CHANCE

DREAM 3
MORNING OF 20 OCTOBER

Bedtime: 3.25 a.m.
Approximate time when fell asleep: 4.10 a.m.
Time awoken: 5.45 a.m.

I am in my room at the Hôtel Saint-Merri and I am dreaming while being fully aware that I am dreaming.

I am waiting for the arrival of my stranger from the steamer, as a bashful lover might wait for his beloved. She won't be much longer. I can feel it, sense it.

Finally, the door opens. Her face is still hidden in the darkness but I know that it's her. She comes into the room. She is even more beautiful than before. Her heart pounds under her dress.

'Who are you?' I ask as she sits down next to me.

Smiling at me, she laces her fingers through mine. Her skin is soft, even softer than I remembered.

'I can't tell you. I do not have the right. But, Andrew, do you really not know?'

I look into her eyes.

'One of those elemental spirits you alluded to on the boat?'

By way of reply, she kisses me with incredible sensuality. I recoil and stare at her again.

'What are these dark forces that are preparing to turn the world upside down? And the train for the east? And the clock showing seven minutes to eight? What do these riddles mean? Tell me, please!'

'Do you believe in me, Andrew?'

'Yes, more than anything.'

'So, prove it to me! Prove it to me tonight! Once our souls have been united, I will be able to answer your questions.'

Immediately, I delicately undo the straps of her dress, which slips to the floor. Her opalescent bosom with its wonderful curves fills me with desire. I take her by the shoulders, gently as if I fear she might break, and she lies down on top of me, her head pressed against mine, her long hair covering my face. At that moment, I have a vision of a torrent of blood boiling in my veins. I feel almost as though I'm suffocating.

Our two bodies are as close as possible to one another. They rise together, in the same rhythm, and cannot stop.

I wake up in a sweat at the peak of pleasure.

NOTES UPON WAKING

1. I no longer feel that overwhelming sense of guilt which has come over me every time I've woken up in the last couple of nights. At the same time, my body remembers (is it proper to admit it?) an extremely intense pleasure.

2. I would like to return immediately to my dreams and find my beautiful stranger. She promised to answer my questions. Will she? But I fear that, in my current state of agitation, sleep will elude me for the rest of the night.

'Here began what I will call the spilling over of the dream into real life,' wrote Nerval in *Aurélia*.

I too felt that the thin barrier between dreams and reality, between daytime and nocturnal life, was breaking down. I was prey to an obsession, about a woman I had only glimpsed and who was taking possession of my nights.

Did the stranger from the steamer exist in real life or had I invented her entirely? If she had only been created by a mirage, how had the medium at the Institut been able to see her? Was she, in fact, one of those legendary succubi from the Middle Ages? These questions continued to go round and round in my head from the time I awoke until the sun rose. They were still clamouring for attention as I sat at the reading table in the hotel lobby and tried to fortify myself with a cup of French coffee and the works of Nerval.

'It has occurred to me many times that, during some important moments in life, a Spirit from another world is suddenly incarnated in the form of an ordinary person and acts or tries to act on us without that ordinary person knowing or remembering.'

I interrupted my reading of *Aurélia* again. Nerval's words so echoed my own experience that images from my dream leapt from the page, bringing with them a new rush of questions. If I had not woken up in the night (or if I had gone back to sleep and managed to continue the dream) would the stranger have shed some light on the situation as she had promised? Above all, were these dreams connected to the Deadly Sleep case?

The previous evening, after James and I had managed to wake Breton from his lethal dream and placed him in the hands of his wife, a doctor and Superintendent Fourier, I had had the unpleasant feeling as we stepped on to the pavement outside 42 Rue Fontaine, utterly exhausted, that I was being watched by an unseen eye. At that time of night the street was almost deserted and the windows of the houses opposite were empty. And yet I could have sworn that *his* gaze, the Austrian's, was on me. There was no need to look behind one of those windows or into the shadow of a carriage entrance, I

136

could feel that he was there, present and absent at the same time. Man or ghost? I didn't know but he was cursing me for foiling his attack.

Like Nerval, I was going mad. My reason was slipping away as his had done.

At that moment James appeared in front of me, freshly shaved. It was almost eleven o'clock. I had not noticed time passing.

'Did you sleep well, my friend?' he asked, clapping me on the back.

'Not really. For the last few nights sleep has become a rare commodity for me.'

'Given current events, that may be a good thing! I slept like a log. Are Fourier and Lacroix here yet?'

I was wondering if it was the right moment to tell my faithful friend about my night-time experiences, since there seemed to be a connection, although still unexplained, with our case, when I noticed the tweed suit and bowler hat of the superintendent, flanked by the svelte figure of the *Paris-Soir* journalist. Not wanting an audience, I decided to put the conversation off for the time being.

As he entered the lobby Lacroix, who was dressed as if he was on his way to a dance, exuded the healthy glow of one who had enjoyed a refreshing night's sleep. Fourier's night had obviously been much shorter.

'I say, your face is even paler than the superintendent's!' said Lacroix, joining us at the table. 'Your night-time exploits must have exhausted you.'

'What … what exploits?' I stammered, troubled by the idea that my lustful dream was written all over my face.

'Why, at Rue Fontaine of course! Fourier has just told me all about it. You saved Breton from certain death, didn't you?'

'It was a close call.'

'By the way, Superintendent, do you know how he is?' asked James.

'The doctor says his condition is satisfactory. As a precaution, he has been transferred to Hôpital Lariboisière for a day or two so that they can carry out some tests.'

'I must congratulate you, gentlemen,' continued the journalist. 'Thanks to you, Breton is safe and sound and he can continue to write his strange little books, at which he so excels, for many years to come.'

'My word!' cried Fourier. 'What does this Austrian do to kill his victims? It really defies comprehension!'

'One explanation might be that he can induce hallucinations while they sleep. That at least is the theory of some of the scientists at the Institut Métapsychique.'

'Hallucinations? From a distance?'

'Why not? Although hypnotism has been recognised by the Faculty for decades, no one has yet managed to understand it fully.'

The superintendent sighed, sitting back heavily in his seat.

'The Doumergue cabinet is in turmoil. It's not yet official but Sarraut has just resigned following the attacks in Marseille. The government is foundering. To keep his head above water, the Justice Minister wants results in the Deadly Sleep case.'

Fourier paused while he compulsively rearranged the single lock of hair on his head.

'We may have managed to save Breton from death but the Austrian is still as elusive as ever. We haven't got the slightest lead.'

'And of course he could always just leave Paris,' I added.

'What do your overseas colleagues have to say, Superintendent?' asked James.

'I haven't had an answer from New York yet. But yesterday I received a cable from the Amsterdam police. An unnamed man, who more or less fits the description of Andreas Eberlin, tried to contact Professor Van Brennen shortly before his death. Unfortunately, the Dutch detectives have no further information about the man. But it does confirm your feeling, Lacroix, that all these cases are connected.'

'I knew it!'

'And the Viennese police?'

'There is no one on their files corresponding to the names or descriptions we gave them. For good reason.'

'The morning papers have not had time to report the story,' continued James. 'If the Austrian thinks that Breton has gone *ad patres*, maybe he will go to the Café de la Place Blanche to make sure.'

'I doubt that our man will go there again,' retorted Fourier. 'I asked the papers to say nothing about last night's incident but I am under no illusions. The news that Breton nearly died is currently spreading around Paris like wildfire.'

'What is to be done then?'

'I have stationed an officer in his room at Lariboisière. Since the stranger wanted him dead and didn't succeed, he'll probably try again. We'll watch the writer day and night while he's there and too bad if Monsieur doesn't like it. I'll do the same when he returns home. I don't think his wife will have any objections.'

'And what if he doesn't turn up again?' I asked.

'Well! Then I fear that he has escaped us for good.'

'What? The deaths of Pierre and the Marquis will go unpunished? No! I will not allow it!' the journalist raged.

'If you have a suggestion, Lacroix, I'm all ears.'

There was an awkward silence. Several times since he had arrived Lacroix had surreptitiously looked at his wristwatch. This time he did so more ostentatiously.

'Twenty-five past eleven already! I'm sorry, gentlemen, I have an appointment which forces me to leave early. Then I intend to think about all this. Yes, *think*! Because there must be a way. I will not give up.'

Lacroix gave a quick bow and left the hotel without further ado.

'Our friend is certainly in a hurry this morning,' said Fourier drily. 'Given his get-up, I'd wager that the reason for his departure has light-brown hair and goes by the name of Amélie de Brindillac. I don't know what they're planning, those two.'

The superintendent picked up his cane and his hat.

'Although it's not the same thing at all, I, too, have an appointment. I am expected at midday by our sleuths at the Préfecture. Between ourselves, it would help me if they have gathered some new information about Ducros's death. After that, I'll get back to the New York Police Department. If necessary, I will demand the intervention of the minister.'

'Lacroix is right,' I speculated, not paying any attention to the superintendent's words. 'There must be a way.'

'Ah, my boy, I'll leave you to your musings! If the truth is revealed, let me know.'

When Fourier had gone, James turned to me.

'It seems that the day has not begun all that well.'

'On the contrary! You wanted to make the most of the City of Light, so you should be happy – we have some time off.'

'Didn't you just say that you wanted to think?'

'No, I said that there must be a way.'

'And how are you going to find it? In books?'

'I think it's time to apply André Breton's theories on chance and necessity to police methods. Or, more precisely, what he calls "objective chance".'

'What?'

In the face of my companion's incomprehension, I seized my copy of *Nadja,* which was still in my bag from the day before, and opened it at a page where the corner had been turned down.

'What I do know,' grumbled James, 'is what it cost us yesterday when you wanted to put Monsieur Breton's lessons into practice. We made fools of ourselves in front of an entire brasserie.'

'It won't be like that this time,' I said, pointing to the sentence I had been looking for. 'It's just a question of letting oneself slide into that – listen to this – "almost forbidden world of sudden parallels, petrifying coincidences, and reflexes peculiar to each individual, of harmonies struck as though on the piano, flashes of light that would make you see, really see, if only they were not so much quicker than all the rest".'

'Sorry, I don't understand any of that gibberish.'

'There's nothing to understand. It just means that we must leave it to Surrealism, be open to the unknown and welcome the mysterious signs which come our way during the day.'

'What?'

'We're going for a walk, James. A walk along the boulevards.'

'Couldn't you have just said that?'

XIV

GOOD NIGHT VIENNA!

It was late October but the weather remained mild, the streets bathed in sunshine.

I had no precise route in mind, no pre-established plan. My only intention was to walk for a long time, a very long time, happy to go where the mood took me, my mind completely open to whatever chance might bring. I enjoyed ambling idly. After wandering aimlessly through the streets for some time, it was as though you developed another sense, allowing you to experience reality differently, revealing unsuspected connections between things, creating space/time relationships outside the bounds of Cartesian reason. In that state of mind, maybe I could re-establish the link with my stranger from the steamer while I was awake.

Having passed Tour Saint-Jacques and crossed the two branches of the Seine, we wandered along Boulevard Saint-Michel. At one of the many bookshops in the area specialising in the occult, I found an edition of *The Key to Black Magic* by Stanislas de Guaïta and Jules Delassus's famous *Incubi and Succubi*. I purchased both books, which joined *Aurélia* and *Nadja* at the bottom of my bag. After making our way through the Luxembourg Gardens, swarming with people on this sunny weekend, we continued to Boulevard du Montparnasse where, on the dot of one o'clock, my sidekick was lured by the promise of a seafood *rémoulade*, and we stopped at La Coupole for some sustenance.

I decided to tell James about my dreams while he made light

work of a trio of chocolate profiteroles accompanied by a smooth ice cream. Then I immediately changed my mind. It was not the right time for discussions, however necessary they were, but for a voyage into the irrational, far from logic and understanding.

We resumed our stroll, this time heading towards Les Invalides. James followed me without grumbling, both amused at the whim which had suddenly taken hold of me and delighted to see me making the most of the splendours of Paris. At the packed pavement cafés, young women with painted nails savoured their Bloody Marys and their champagne, lapping up the glances of the young men around them. Every now and then we passed newspaper kiosks but the grim headlines about the repercussions of the assassination of the King of Yugoslavia in Marseille and the anti-Semitic decrees issued by the new German Führer barely tempered the carefree mood which seemed to be de rigueur in the French capital.

I walked with my eyes wide open, drinking in everything that was going on around me, trying to decipher all the messages reality was sending me. I scrutinised the street signs and examined the slogans of the giant advertising boards on the outside of buildings, looking for hidden meaning. I made up complicated formulae from the omnibus and tram numbers. I spoke the names of shops and cafés out loud as if they had magical significance. I interpreted the positions of the hands on the clocks. I probed the faces of passers-by, firmly convinced that the truth was to be found somewhere, written on the wind of the daily drama of that modern city.

At the Gare d'Orsay we leapt on to an omnibus which was heading for the Champ-de-Mars. It dropped us under the legs of Eiffel's masterpiece. We then crossed the Seine to Trocadéro and headed for Boulevard Haussmann. After walking from Chaussée d'Antin to the Gare du Nord, the Machiavellian gaze of the main character on a poster at Univers Ciné caught my attention and I suggested that we get our strength back by responding to the call of the cinema[15].

'Did you see Mabuse's eyes!' exclaimed James as we came out later.

'Yes. Öberlin's must look like that. It's a sign we are on the right track.'

As daylight began to fade, another omnibus took us from the Gare de l'Est to the Buttes-Chaumont park where we wandered for a long time, looking for a sign, whatever it might be. On the bend in a steep path, James suddenly stopped in front of a noticeboard giving the history of the park.

'There was a gallows on this very spot until the reign of Louis XVI: the gallows of Montfaucon. Does that have anything to do with the author of that book you took from Château B——?'

'Montfaucon de Villars? I don't think so. But it might be a warning. Let's keep going before the garden closes!'

A little further on, we came to the area around the lake and the island where, under a cloudy sky and an almost full moon, my gaze was drawn to the temple of Sibyl at the top of a rocky cliff. Although the water in the lake at the foot of the spur was stagnant, unlike the turbulent waters of the sparkling blue-tinted river, and this was not a castle of old stone but a modern replica of the Tivoli temple, it definitely recalled the mirage of *fata Morgana*.

The medium's words came back to me.

'James! Do you remember what Pfizer said at the Institut Métapsychique?'

'What? That crank?'

'He said: "A train heading east! A train you must not miss!"'

'Yes, I remember. So?'

'He also mentioned a clock face …'

'Yes, it showed seven minutes to eight in the evening. But there's no doubt he's got a screw loose.'

'Where do trains going east leave Paris from?'

'The Gare de l'Est I think.'

'What time is it?'

'Twenty past seven.'

'Quick, we must hurry!'

'What's going on? Will you just tell me?'

'There's no time, James!'

At the northern exit of the park, we leapt into a taxi. Luckily, we didn't have far to go. The driver sped towards the La Villette roundabout and then headed down Rue du Faubourg-Saint-Martin to Place Verdun. In less than ten minutes we were at the great Parisian station. It was almost completely dark.

'Quick! Follow me!'

I crossed the concourse at a run and looked around for a porter.

'Is there a train which leaves at seven minutes to eight?' I gasped.

'Three times a week, Monsieur. And today, Saturday, is one of those days.'

'Which one is it?'

'Over there, Platform 2, the one with the blue-and-gold carriages. It's the Orient Express.'

'The Orient Express?'

'Yes, Monsieur. It arrived earlier today from Calais.'

'And where is it going?'

'Stuttgart, Munich, Salzburg, Vienna, Budapest, Bucharest—'

'Vienna you say?'

'Yes, Vienna.'

'We absolutely must catch that train!' I cried, turning to James who was looking rather taken aback.

'There are usually still seats available at this time of year,' said the porter. 'Go to the ticket studyof the Compagnie Internationale des Wagons-Lits, under the arches, and then find one of the uniformed conductors on the platform[16]. But hurry, the Orient Express will be leaving soon – and it's rarely late.'

The Orient Express! I didn't have enough money on me to pay for such expensive seats but we had to catch that train! It was suddenly clear to me that this was what I had been looking for.

'Are you sure about this, Andrew?'

'Definitely. Our man is on that train. We're going to get him this time.'

'Right, let's warn Fourier so that he can organise a search of the carriages!'

'Out of the question! If the train stays in the station Öberlin will get suspicious and give us the slip again.'

'Damn!' swore my friend as he grudgingly took a thick wallet from his jacket pocket. 'Take that! You'll find my passport inside and a wad of notes! It's all the money I withdrew in London before leaving. I thought I'd squander it on seeing the sights of Paris, not the view from a train window … even if it is aboard the Orient Express!'

I grabbed his wallet and ran to the ticket office. A few minutes later I went up to the uniformed conductor of the first sleeping car and proudly held out the precious tickets.

'I will also need your passports.'

'Here.'

'Very good, Messieurs. You will be in a second-class compartment, couchettes 8 and 9,' announced the conductor, stamping the numbers on his plan. 'Do you have any luggage?'

'Here,' I lied, showing my bag full of books. 'The rest is waiting for us in Vienna.'

'In that case, please get in. The train will leave in less than a minute. Your compartment is at the end of the third carriage. If you wish, you may use the restaurant car. It opens in quarter of an hour.'

A whistle blew; behind us a voice cried: 'All aboard!'

As I mounted the step I had the unpleasant sensation of being watched by terrible, threatening dark eyes. It was the same feeling I had had when we left André Breton's studio the night before.

I craned my neck to try to see *his* face. But it was time for saying goodbye and a number of people were poking their heads out of the carriage windows to bid farewell to those who remained on the platform.

A new blast of whistles was heard. James leapt into the carriage and the conductor followed suit.

Before the conductor closed the door, I took *Nadja* out of my bag, tore out the endpaper and scrawled a few words and my signature on it. Then I hailed a porter whose cap bore the insignia of the Compagnie des Wagons-Lits and gave him the folded piece of paper as well as some money from James's bundle of notes.

'Take this message to Superintendent Fourier at the Sûreté Nationale. It is extremely important. Do you hear? Superintendent Fourier! The Sûreté Nationale!'

The conductor pulled the door towards him and pushed down the safety latch.

'Well, it's good night Vienna for us!' I exclaimed, giving James back his wallet minus an appreciable number of notes. 'There's no going back now.'

'*Good night Vienna!*' cried my friend.

The Orient Express rumbled off slowly, spitting out steam.

In a little over twenty hours we would be in the Austrian capital.

XV

ALL ABOARD THE ORIENT EXPRESS

'"Dark forces which are preparing to turn the world upside down?"' repeated James after I had told him about my dreams, although underplaying their erotic charge. 'What does it mean?'

'I don't know yet. All I know is that these dreams follow on from one another and contain a message which it's important I understand. It started with the mirage on the *Canterbury*. My dream last night was part of it, as was, of course, the medium's vision.'

We were sitting comfortably on a mahogany-framed banquette in our compartment. Outside the window, landscapes cloaked in darkness sped past under a starry sky.

'And if it is a message, who is sending it to you? That woman? And who is she? The spirit of a dead person? One of those sylphids they mention in your book, *Le Comte of what's-his-name?*'

'*Le Comte de Gabalis*. Yes, at the moment I am convinced she is a kind of elemental spirit.'

'Golly! If I were to be visited by one of those creatures, well, I'd sleep all the time. Is she pretty?'

'If you'd read Joris-Karl Huysmans you'd know a bit more about their powers of seduction.'

'Sorry, I haven't had the pleasure of discovering that gentleman's work.'

'He was a French writer. He died a quarter of a century ago. He discussed the theme of succubi extensively in a novel called *Là-bas*. He was loyal to the ancient demonologists and saw them as satanic creatures. But it was a serious subject for him, not be taken lightly. He had personal experience of it when he stayed in the Trappist monastery of Notre Dame d'Igny.'

'My word! How I envy you two, you and this Huysmans chap.'

'In any case, since I became open to the possibility of communicating via the gates of sleep, things have become clearer.'

'Well, as you can see, I am delighted! Here we are, stuck on a train on the basis of a hunch and our Austrian friend might still be running around the streets of Paris.'

'It's not a hunch, James. Pfizer's words put me on the right track. And don't forget that Öberlin's return was planned. It was explicitly referred to in the telegram found at La Toison d'Or.'

'The telegram said the 23rd and it's only the 20th today. Why would he have decided to go back today in particular? And why take this train? His plot against Breton failed. It doesn't seem like him to leave without finishing the job.'

'No doubt he had more important things to do.'

There was a knock at the door.

'Come in!' called James.

It was the conductor of our carriage.

'Messieurs, the final sitting is about to start in the restaurant.'

'Ah! A very timely reminder!' said my friend. 'I am dying of hunger.'

The man in the blue uniform prepared to close the door but I rose and held out my hand to stop him.

'How many carriages does this train have?'

'Six, Monsieur. There are three sleeping cars, a restaurant car and two wagons, one at the front and one at the back, where the equipment is stored.'

'Are the sleeping cars all in the same section?'

'No. The third one is after the restaurant car. It was added at the

Gare de l'Est and will be uncoupled at Budapest. Only the other two will go on to Romania.'

'At this time I imagine that most of the passengers are in the restaurant car.'

'I doubt it, Monsieur. There have already been several sittings since we left Paris! You are among the last to dine.'

'Ah, I see. One last thing, how many passengers are on the train?'

'Unless I am mistaken, five compartments are empty: three singles in first class and two doubles in second class. In other words seven empty beds. The train can take up to forty-eight passengers. So that makes forty-one with the seven empty beds.'

'Forty-one! Very precise! Thank you.'

'At your service, Messieurs.'

The man left. James pulled me towards the restaurant car. In the corridor I took the opportunity to have a good look at the faces of the dozen or so passengers we passed. Amongst them were couples and single passengers: English, French, Italians, Germans, Austrians and Hungarians who were striking up conversations in a surprising mixture of European languages. Only the upper echelons of society were represented (financiers, well-to-do people, aristocrats, intellectuals, artists, etc.) but none of them looked anything like the individual we sought.

When we entered the restaurant we were welcomed deferentially by the head waiter who sat us at a table for two.

The carriage was only about a third full at that time in the evening. During the course of the meal (which was, incidentally, exquisite and served with an excellent Moselle wine), a very forthcoming waiter with a Swiss accent told us all about our neighbours.

Next to us were Herr Hersteinmeyer, the great banker from Munich, Frau Hersteinmeyer and a servant; at the table behind me sat Countess Dravidia who was returning to her estate in the St Pölten region with her young secretary; next to them chatting happily, were Miss Denbar and Miss Arianovski, inseparable elderly ladies on a European tour; next to them smoking an impressive cigar was a man reading the newspaper. He was the retired General von Bülow. According to the waiter, the soldier was attempting to exorcise the trauma of the German surrender and signing of the armistice in restaurant car No. 2419 of the Compagnie Internationale des Wagons-Lits on 11 November 1918 by spending most of his pension haunting the trains of the Belgian company between Paris, Vienna and Berlin.

On the other side of the carriage, behind my friend, was the table of Mademoiselle Ida Petrini, a Franco-Italian actress of whom neither James nor I had heard; she was accompanied by her impresario who was making it a point of honour to talk loudly and with his mouth full, boasting of the starlet's flourishing success. Further away, just finishing his meal, sat Mr Boormann, a successful American writer who was returning to the old Austro-Hungarian Empire to gather material for a new romantic novel. At the very end of the carriage were four young English academics going to Salzburg for a conference at Mozarteum University. They were immersed in a passionate debate. Just before the door to the kitchens was Mademoiselle Lisa Dampierre, a Parisian painter of about forty, accompanied by her maidservant.

There were exactly seventeen passengers in the carriage. If they were added to the fifteen we had passed in the corridor to reach the dining car, it made thirty-two passengers out of a total of forty-one. And still no sign of the Austrian.

A few minutes earlier Mademoiselle Dampierre had opened a book and begun reading avidly.

'I would love to know what that young lady is reading,' I mused out loud.

'If you would allow me, Monsieur,' said the waiter, bringing two glasses of a vintage cognac we had ordered, 'Mademoiselle Dampierre is reading *The Interpretation of Dreams* by Professor Sigmund Freud.'

'Dreams! Dreams again!' muttered James before putting the glass to his lips.

'Indeed, I believe I am right in saying that Mademoiselle Dampierre is going to Vienna to meet the famous doctor.'

'Did she tell you that?' I asked, surprised.

'No. But when she is not absorbed in that book, she continually rereads a letter sent from 19 Bergasse, Vienna IX. That is the professor's address.'

'You seem well informed.'

'Oh, she's not the first and she won't be the last of that gentleman's patients to take the Orient Express. I have been working on this line for ten years and I have come across several from France, England and America. Like Mademoiselle Dampierre, they spend the entire journey studying the great man's work. You'd think they were sitting an examination. On the outward journey they are all silent, like this lady.'

'And on the return journey?'

'That depends. Some seem satisfied, others look even more depressed than when they left.'

'You would have made an excellent detective.'

The waiter thanked me with a bow, keeping his tray flat.

As he went into the kitchens the train slowed down and pulled into Nancy station.

'One of us should go on to the platform to see which passengers get off,' said James, looking out of the window. 'If you're right and our chap is on the train, there's nothing to say that he won't break his journey here.'

'Our man is going to Vienna, James. I'm sure of it. There really is no reason for him to get off here.'

Herr and Frau Hersteinmeyer had returned to their compartment and I caught the attention of the waiter, who was busy clearing their table.

'Do you know the name of an Austrian passenger travelling alone who has very strange eyes? We met him on the platform earlier at the Gare de l'Est. We would very much like to talk to him again.'

'A passenger with strange eyes? Hmm! Sorry, I don't know who you mean.'

'Really? Have all the passengers eaten in the restaurant car this evening?'

'No, Monsieur. Three passengers have remained in their compartments.'

'Aha!' I said, kicking James's leg under the table.

Stubbornly sticking to his plan, James was staring intently at the platform. He had to admit there was very little happening out there. In front of our window the conductor of one of the sleeping cars was chatting to the station master. Not far away five or six passengers had got off to stretch their legs and smoke in the cool Lorraine night.

'Maybe the man I'm talking about is one of those passengers,' I continued.

'It could be the man in Compartment 3, Herr Kessling, in the middle carriage. He got on at Paris and I think he is going to Vienna. The other two are a Madame Blattensohn, a rich English widow, and her daughter who are going to Bratislava. I doubt you mean them.'

'Herr Kessling you say?'

'That's right.'

'And you haven't seen him?'

'No.'

The waiter moved away.

'Did you hear that, James? Compartment 3, the middle carriage.'

'Well! I think we should see for ourselves. Let's go and knock on his door!'

'Absolutely not! We should be as discreet as possible.'

'What do you suggest then?'

'It's a long way to Vienna. Hunger will force him out of his lair. Let's wait until tomorrow.'

The station master blew the whistle for departure. The conductor and the passengers returned to their carriages and the train pulled out with a screech of steel, clouds of steam swirling past our window.

No passengers had left the train and no new passengers had got on.

My watch showed that it was a quarter to one. Since the stop at Nancy station the restaurant had emptied. We decided that it was time to go back to our compartment too.

In the next carriage the corridor was completely deserted, apart from the conductor sitting on his stool reading the newspaper.

We returned the conductor's greeting and continued along the corridor, pausing in front of Compartment 3. What wouldn't we have given to see through the polished wooden door! To finally find out what that monster looked like. To see his face.

As the conductor was looking at us curiously, I pushed James forward and we went back to our compartment.

On entering, we were pleased to note that the beds had been made up. The seat had been turned into a bed and an upper bunk had been folded out from behind a panel.

I undressed quickly and threw myself on the bottom bunk. I was so exhausted that I put down my copy of *Aurélia* after only a few pages.

For the first time in several nights I didn't feel terrified of going to sleep. On the contrary, I was desperate for my consciousness to be suspended, to find that place, so near and yet so far, where (as I had only understood that day) lines could be drawn between the invisible planes of reality. The day had reconciled me to my dreams and it was from them above all that I expected further enlightenment – from them and from my stranger.

It was a quarter past one when I fell asleep, rocked by the swaying of the carriages. However, for what seemed like an age, my sleep was too disjointed for dreams to take shape.

On the upper bunk, James kept turning over. When the train stopped at the next station (Strasbourg probably, unless I had missed one) I saw him quickly climb down from his bed and disappear into the corridor. I had no idea what time it was.

I had barely begun to enter the phase of active dreams when a jolt of the train woke me with a start. Shortly after Strasbourg, the train seemed to slow down again. Half asleep, I could just hear the voice of the conductor advising a passenger that it was nothing, only German customs at the Kehl border in the Baden region.

Was it because we had now entered the land of National Socialism that I began to see a series of rambling visions of Hitler's face and his dark army of Blackshirts?

Over the last few months the press had given a lot of coverage to the Führer's decree that non-Aryan people should henceforth be forced out of public office. It had left no doubt about his Greater Germany project, a vast empire where inferior races and classes would be excluded. Similarly, the day after the Night of the Long Knives on 30 June the newspapers had been quick to condemn the bloody purge of the *Sturmabteilung*.

A noise in the compartment drove these troubling scenes from my mind. James must have gone back to bed earlier without me noticing because, opening one eye, I now saw him leave our compartment again and gently close the door.

I made no attempt to understand what he was up to and went straight back to sleep.

That was when I had a terrible dream, the venomous nature of which I have never forgotten; a nightmare which, masquerading as truth, began at the very moment when I thought I was waking up. It was as if dreams and reality, daytime and nocturnal life, had become one for me.

DREAM 4
NIGHT OF 20–21 OCTOBER

Bedtime: 1.05 a.m.
Approximate time when fell asleep: 1.15 a.m.
Time awoken: 4.55 a.m. (Central European Time)

I am stretched out on my bed, my thoughts all over the place. I feel that I have been thrown on to the shores of sleep by a wave of dreams with neither beginning nor end, dreams which became entangled and whose memory is already fading.

I am not sure I am completely awake but I don't think I am asleep either. I have the strange impression that I am floating in a sort of in-between place, an intermediate and worrying state. My eyes are wide open... at least I think they are.

The regular rocking movement reminds me that I am on a train. Although the compartment is cloaked in darkness, I recognise the panelling of the walls, the designs on the marquetry and the white enamel basin. The scents of metal, wood and velvet mingle in the air.

Suddenly, I detect a movement close to me and at the same time I have the very clear impression that someone is there. Is it my stranger come to visit me? No, I cannot see her opalescent aura. It is more like a diffused feeling of imminent danger. A lurking threat. Ready to pounce.

It is only at that moment that I become aware of my true situation. My arms, legs and all the muscles in my body are turned to stone. I am unable to move, totally paralysed. Only my eyelids still function.

Fear grabs me by the throat. At the same time, my head is filled with a high-pitched shrieking like a small animal. Is it the sound of the train screeching round a bend? Or the distorted echo of my pulse which is thumping like the beat of a drum? My hoarse breathing burning my lungs? But I am sure that it is not coming from me. So who from? Every passing second strengthens my conviction that there is a hostile presence near me.

Again, I feel that something is moving in the compartment. With all my energy I try to lift my head to determine where the danger is coming from but I cannot. Out of the corner of my eye I just manage to glimpse the outline of a stocky body, no more than three foot tall – a child? A monkey? It has extraordinary strength; it throws itself on me and crushes my chest.

After my aggressor has thrown me backwards with a violent blow, my head is crushed against the wall. In that position I cannot see it. I would have liked to look at it, to express my incomprehension, my hostility, my hatred. But even speaking or moaning is impossible; no sound comes out of my mouth.

The smell of its skin repulses me. A damp odour of decay and wet hair. I am certain that I am experiencing the last moments of my life. There is no hope. All I can do is wait. I am frightened.

With its full weight on me, the creature grabs my neck and begins to squeeze. A trickle of acrid bile rises in my throat. Despite the brutality of the attack, I do not feel any pain. My body is anaesthetised.

I am finding it increasingly hard to breathe. I close my eyes. While death takes hold of me with all its might, a vague image of the stranger from the steamer, in her red satin dress, forms in my mind.

I am intoxicated by the memory of her radiant face. A feeling of relief.

Fear releases its grip.

'You must believe in me, Andrew. Your life depends on it.'

'Yes,' I hear myself reply. 'More than in anything.'

Thanks to her, the strength to fight reawakens in me. I unclench my teeth, pull in my stomach and chest and, in a final burst of energy, manage to expel a powerful, guttural, primitive cry from the depths of my being.

Immediately, I hear noises in the corridor. There is a blinding light. I cover my eyes with my hands.

I am roughly shaken by the shoulders.

A voice.

'Wake up, Andrew! Wake up!'

James's face ...

What would have happened if my friend had not come back then? If my stranger from the steamer had not appeared? Was that the fear the Marquis de Brindillac had felt before he died? And the others?

I had the ghastly feeling of having come back from the dead. My face, my neck, my chest bore no scars. All I had seen in the dream was only an illusion. And yet, that illusion had almost killed me.

The conductor of the sleeping car appeared a few seconds after James. When I had managed to convince him that I was as well as could be expected, the conductor went to reassure the passengers in the neighbouring compartments who had been unceremoniously woken by my cry.

Then I gave James a thorough account of my dream.

'Do you really think that it's Öberlin ...or rather, Kessling, who's doing this?' he asked, sitting on the edge of my bed.

'I am more convinced than ever.'

'My word! How is he doing it?'

'I don't know. But I can assure you that we have been lucky. If you ad stayed in the compartment you would certainly have received he same treatment and neither of us would be here to tell the tale.'

James couldn't help shuddering as he imagined the possibility.

The brakes of the Orient Express screeched as we pulled into a tation. The blind was lowered so we couldn't see its name. In any ase, we were too shaken, both of us, to take anything in.

'I couldn't stop thinking about Kessling,' confided my friend. I was only afraid of one thing – that he might give us the slip at one of the stops. In Strasbourg and then Kehl I went to check that he hadn't got out. But there was no sound from his compartment. Everything seemed quiet. I even thought for a moment that you might have been mistaken, Andrew, and that our man was not even on the Orient Express. After Kehl I stayed in the corridor chatting to the conductor. That was when I heard your cry.'

A whistle sounded on the platform.

'At least we can be sure of one thing now,' he muttered. 'The Austrian is on the train!'

Suddenly, James ran to the window as if a snake had bitten him and he raised the blind.

'What's happening?'

'Baden-Oos!' he roared. 'The train has stopped at the station of Baden-Oos! What a fool I am!'

It was only then that the gravity of the situation dawned on me. Luckily, my friend had enough energy for both of us. He threw himself out of the compartment and ran as quickly as possible towards the other carriage.

I didn't have the strength to follow him. I collapsed on the bed, my hands covering my face, praying that it was not too late, but James had barely left our carriage before the train began to move again.

A few minutes later he returned, looking shaken.

'He got away, didn't he?'

'When I arrived the door was open and the compartment was empty. In the time it took me to leap on to the platform, he had already disappeared.'

'Did anyone see him?'

'The conductor.'

'Did he say what he looked like?'

'About fifty, five foot eight, short hair combed back, greying temples. Kessling had come flying out of his compartment, a suitcase in his hand. He was barely dressed. The conductor confirmed that he should have stayed on board until Vienna.'

'Nothing else?'

'Yes. He had puffy eyes, a wild look, like someone who had just woken up.'

'What? Kessling had just woken up?'

'Apparently.'

It was only quarter past five in the morning but, for James and me, going back to sleep was out of the question. Until we had removed the threat of this sinister character, the gates of sleep would be barred; our lives were at risk if we ventured beyond them.

We had to keep going. We knew that Kessling was heading for Vienna and that was where we would catch him. That day, the next day or another day.

About twenty minutes later, the train stopped at Karlsruhe station.

When the Orient Express arrived at Westbahnhof in Vienna on Sunday 21 October 1934 it was half past six in the evening.

XVI

THE NEED FOR SLEEP

Beautiful Vienna! City of the Habsburgs. Capital of arts and music. City of Brahms, Bruckner, Mahler and Schönberg. Klimt and Schiele. Hofmannsthal, Schnitzler, Zweig. Fritz Lang and Freud.

But sinister Vienna too. A gigantic metropolis where the new Führer had spent his youth and honed his racist doctrines. The centre of Pan-Germanism, nationalist leagues and sickening theories.

The previous July, with the support of the Third Reich, the local Nazis had attempted *a coup d'etat*. The Austrian Chancellor, Engelbert Dollfuss, had been murdered along with hundreds of other people, but it had ended in failure. Dollfuss himself, although opposed to the Nazis, was no better than them. Under his reign Austria had become an authoritarian regime, the right to strike and gather had been removed, and the leaders of opposition parties forced to seek exile. The Chancellor who replaced him was cut from the same cloth.

Dark forces preparing to turn the world upside down!

Outside the station the air was heavy, the sky black. It was pouring with rain. The streetlamps had not been lit and in the distance, towards the Danube, monstrous shadows were lengthening over the old city. Immediately, I was seized with a premonition similar to the one I had had the day after I arrived in Paris when I had leant on the parapet of the Pont-au-Change, contemplating the river. This time the feeling was even stronger.

We needed to find a place to stay quickly and come up with a plan.

James hailed a taxi and we jumped in to escape the rain.

'We're looking for a hotel,' explained my friend, miming to the driver. 'Not ruinously expensive. Comfortable.'

'*Bitte schön?*'

'Hotel! Sleep! *Schlaffen!*'

'*Ach, ja! Hotel Regina. Freiheit Platz.*'

And the taxi set off.

'Well, sleeping is one way of putting it!' I sighed.

The hotel was extremely comfortable but not exactly cheap. Located close to Ringstrasse, opposite the neogothic Votivkirche, it was popular with tourists.

It was still raining heavily in the Austrian capital. As we had no desire to wander through the city's streets to find somewhere cheaper to stay, we went inside. The tickets for the Orient Express had not exhausted James's reserves. We had enough to last a few days.

The receptionist seemed suspicious of us – foreigners without luggage asking for a double room – but finally decided to give us a key.

The room was pleasant and looked out over Votivkirche Square.

While James freshened up in the bathroom, I stretched out and, to avoid nodding off to sleep, got *Aurélia* out of my bag and skimmed the first paragraph. I knew every sentence by heart: 'Our dreams are a second life. Never have I been able to pass without a shudder through those gates of ivory or horn which divide us from the invisible world. The first moments of sleep are the image of death: a hazy torpor overcomes our thoughts, and it is impossible for us to determine the precise instant when the I, in another form, resumes the creative work of existence. Little by little an obscure underground cavern grows lighter, and the pale, solemnly immobile figures that inhabit the realm of limbo emerge from shadows and darkness. Then the picture takes shape, a new light illumines and sets in motion these odd apparitions: the world of Spirits opens before us.'

Raising my eyes to the only window, where the Viennese night could be seen between the thick yellow curtains of the hotel room, I ran through my memories of dreams. I, too, had seen one of those pale figures appear from the other side of the gates of sleep on several occasions. Who was she? What did she want with me? What was her name?

Nerval then began a patient description of what he called his long illness which he had spent entirely among the vagaries of the mind: 'A lady of whom I had long been fond and whom I shall call Aurélia was lost to me,' he wrote. 'Condemned by the one I loved, guilty of a mistake for which I no longer hoped to be forgiven, it only remained for me to throw myself into vulgar intoxications. I affected joy and cheerfulness. I crossed the world, madly in love with variety and caprice. Above all, I loved the costumes and the strange morals of distant populations. It seemed that I could thereby shift the conditions of good and evil.'

The writer based his work on his own experience. I had discovered from reading Aristide Marie's biography that the Aurélia in question was really called Jenny Colon, an actress with whom Nerval had been madly in love. But in 1838 she had married someone else and Nerval had come to Vienna to lick his wounds. He had lived in the Austrian capital from 19 November 1839 until 1 March 1840, staying at the Aigle Noir inn in the suburb of Leopoldstadt.

I looked up at the yellow curtains again and my thoughts swirled above the two spires of the Votivkirche which were suddenly illuminated.

Without my realising it, by leaving Paris for the banks of the Danube the link with Gérard de Nerval had not been broken. On the contrary, I was still following his path. Inexorably.

At about half past nine in the evening we came down from our room.

In the lobby I sent a short telegram to the French Sûreté, addressed to Superintendent Edmond Fourier, to tell him the name of our hotel. I then bought a map of the city and a few French newspapers: *Paris-Soir*, *L'Excelsior* and *Le Petit Parisien*.

Outside it had stopped raining but the air was much cooler than in Paris.

We walked down Herrengasse and then wandered through the old streets of the city centre to Graben and Stephansplatz.

The night promised to be long. The fact that we had no idea how the Austrian induced nightmares in his victims meant that we had to tread very carefully. Neither James nor I wanted to fall into the hands of Morpheus. We would have to kill time, hour after hour, until the sun came up.

Another consequence of the situation was that communication with my stranger was suspended until further notice. It was impossible to obtain new information through her.

Not far from the cathedral, we went into a smoky tavern on Bauernmarkt where a plump, blonde waitress wearing a strange Hungarian hat stuffed James with sausages and mutton chops while I just had a few *Knödel* and a meat soup.

After the meal I took a look at the newspapers I had bought at the hotel. They were from the day before and the news was not very up to date. *Paris-Soir* (whose report was not the work of a certain J.L.; Lacroix had apparently kept his promise to be discreet) and *Le Petit Parisien* discussed the *affaire* of Deadly Sleep in depth. The news of a second investigation into the death of Ducros had just been made public and journalists were focusing on the political repercussions of events. As Fourier had predicted, the attack on the leader of the Surrealists was mentioned, as were our own names.

At half past midnight we left the tavern and wandered through the city in a north-easterly direction. We crossed the Donaukanal, strolled around the Praterstern monument and the Augarten park area and then returned to the city centre via the long Taborstrasse (the street where Nerval had lived nearly a century earlier).

In the end, we began to feel terribly tired. Oh sleep! Sleep! It seemed a long time since I had had the luxury of an entire night's rest (not since leaving London actually). At that moment, how I would have liked to fall into a deep sleep!

A crazy idea which would considerably improve our situation came to me when we were on Schwedenbrücke after crossing the Donaukanal again.

I remembered the words of Monsieur de Vallemont, the vice-chairman of the Institut Métapsychique, about one of the Marquis de Brindillac's discoveries: 'Dreams occupy a small part of the time devoted to sleep; they only appear about *an hour and a half* after we fall asleep and then return regularly in brief sequences.'

If the good Marquis was to be believed, the gates of sleep would only open intermittently and, moreover, regularly and predictably. When they were closed dreams could not develop. Nothing therefore prevented James and me from getting some rest as long as we took turns and, above all, shook the sleeper awake before he started dreaming.

Nonetheless, should Auguste de Brindillac's theories be accepted without question? What had he based his ideas on?

From the jumble of memories from my reading, a passage from *De natura rerum* came to me in which Lucretius confirmed that while they slept domestic dogs and goats always gave little uncontrolled jolts, an unmistable sign of dream activity.

If the Latin philosopher had been right (and if the idea could be applied to humans) dreaming produced physical effects on people.

Maybe the Marquis de Brindillac had developed his audacious principle by observing these physical effects. To be certain, it should be enough to imitate the scientist and observe a sleeping person; if he demonstrated rapid and unconscious movements at one time or another, it must mean that he was actively dreaming.

I put my idea to James. He seemed very sceptical but, in the absence of anything else and wanting to have a rest as much as I did, he agreed to try the experiment.

At about half past one in the morning we returned to our room.

James lay down on his bed, fully dressed, and without further ado he fell asleep.

Sitting in an armchair next to him, I smoked cigarette after cigarette in an attempt to fight off drowsiness.

At three o'clock, an hour and a half after he had fallen asleep, his body was still just as serene. Apart from two or three changes in position and sustained snoring, there was nothing of note.

Clearly, the experiment was not conclusive. It would have been reckless to take it any further.

I was therefore preparing to wake him when his breathing suddenly accelerated, his fingers moved on the sheet as if he was playing the piano and his eyes, until then tightly shut, opened almost entirely and I noticed that they were rolling wildly. The effect was striking[16]. I immediately shook James roughly by the shoulder. He stared at me for a few seconds, stunned, and then, pulling himself together, confessed that he had just started having a dream which promised to be very amusing.

I was delighted. Not only did dreaming have an effect on the body of the sleeper but it was perfectly visible. We could recover from our exhaustion without any risk.

That night we swapped places on the bed several times for periods of ninety minutes each.

Just before the Votivkirche bell tolled seven times the following morning I shook my friend excitedly.

'James! James! Wake up! I think I've discovered how Kessling kills his victims!'

'Really?' he groaned, his eyes half closed with sleep. 'Would it be by tormenting people like you do?'

He sat on the edge of the bed and looked towards the window.

'The sun isn't even up yet! Couldn't you have let me sleep a bit longer?'

'It was my turn anyway. But listen to this!'

The books I had bought two days ago on Boulevard Saint-Michel were open on my lap and I had circled certain passages in pencil.

'In here,' I said, pointing to Jules Delassus's essay, 'it says that observers can interfere with the psyche of a sleeping subject from a distance. To do so, they fall asleep voluntarily and then leave their own bodies, creating a kind of ghost which can take any shape and any possible or imaginable face.'

'Aha! A hallucination then.'

'If you like, but not a hallucination as understood today, James. The nightmare which took hold of me in our compartment on the Orient Express was not just a dream. The horrible creature which tried to kill me had a tangible existence on another plane of reality, the one which provides access to the gates of sleep several times during the night. It was created in the mind of Herr Kessling.'

'Very well, but how does he cause death? In principle, unless your heart is very weak, you do not die of fear.'

'A sleeping person is naturally in a vulnerable mental state. All Kessling, or rather the creature created by him, has to do is break the thin invisible thread which connects the various planes of the personality in order to kill the sleeper in a few seconds. The look of terror which all the victims displayed can be explained like this: a psychic entity had become master of their consciousness and all they could do was witness their own death with fear. As effective as a bullet straight through the heart.'

'And it leaves no trace.'

'Indeed. In so doing, Kessling has almost managed to perfect a new kind of crime in a locked room. When it has been established that all the exits from the scene of the tragedy are hermetically sealed, no police officer will think of the door to dreams.'

'So he went after all those specialist dream researchers to prevent them discovering the secret?'

'Probably. As long as it remained confined to obscure essays on the occult, to which no one *serious* has paid any attention in our time, there was no risk. On the other hand, if a famous scientist discovered the existence of the gates of sleep and decided to talk about it with anyone ready to listen it would become dangerous. I strongly suspect that, within the context of his work on lucid dreams, the Marquis de Brindillac was very close to solving the mystery. That is probably what he was preparing to reveal in his lecture.'

'And your little Tinker Bell, what has she to do with all this?' asked James, rubbing his face to wake himself up.

'To tell you the truth, I don't really know. These books say that elemental spirits rarely intervene in human affairs. That is why their existence inspires such caution. There must be a compelling reason for her to do so.'

'It could be the death of the poor Marquis.'

'Possibly. But it would seem that an even more terrible secret is hidden behind all these deaths.'

'More terrible than the possibility of being bumped off by an invisible power while you sleep? I really don't see what!'

James stood up and went to the bathroom. For a few minutes

I heard the gush of water from the tap. When he reappeared with a towel over his shoulder and his face and shirt collar wet, he no longer looked befuddled and was smiling broadly. The strength of character and cheerful temperament of my friend, who was always ready to see the lighter side of things, were a constant source admiration to me.

'My word! I have known more peaceful dreams!'

Sitting down on the bed again, he looked at me mockingly.

'Tell me one thing, dear friend. If your stranger from the steamer really is one of those alluring spirits who haunt the hidden corners of nature, why has she chosen you to deliver her messages? If she was looking for a good-looking young detective, able to save the world from evil powers who want to destroy it, why not choose me?'

'Oh! I don't doubt for an instant that you were her first choice!' I exclaimed, laughing. 'But I think that one crucial thing influenced her decision.'

'Oh yes? What might that be?'

'Nerval.'

'Nerval?'

'Yes. I am convinced that my desire to solve the mystery of his death created a sympathetic link with the occult.'

'Are you saying that this beauty knew your poet?'

'Gérard's spirit would often wander through the invisible world, putting his mental state at risk. No doubt he formed a number of relationships and was liked and appreciated by ethereal people.'

'Hmm, I see! Nerval's friends are their friends. So, don't forget to remind them that I am your friend, Andrew! If I'm lucky, a succubus with a fantastic body will visit me too!'

He threw his towel into the middle of the room with a chuckle.

'Well? What are we doing today?' he asked when he had stopped laughing.

'Let's concentrate on the information provided by my stranger. In particular, I am convinced that the castle with the pointed roof, which appeared in my vision on the *Canterbury*, is an essential clue. That is where we should go.'

'A castle with a pointed roof? It's not much of a clue.'

'Except that it was only one element of a larger picture, a magnificent steep valley cut by a river with blue water, probably the Danube.'

I put the two books on the occult on the bed and went over to the large cupboard which took up half the wall. I opened the drawers and pulled out a tourist leaflet which I held out to my friend, open at the relevant page.

'I found this brochure when I was looking for something to write on last night. A guest must have left it behind, unless the hotel management puts a copy in every room.'

'The Wachau valley! That is what your vision was? Are you sure?'

'There's no doubt about it. The Wachau starts in Melk and ends in Krems, east of Vienna. It is a very well-known local attraction. I've looked carefully at the photograph. It's the same landscape of vines, conifers and oak trees that I saw in the vision. Its eighteen miles contain a considerable number of ruined monasteries, fortresses and eyries perched on the rocks. We just have to find the one we're looking for.'

'And how do we get to this haven of splendour?'

'Look at the brochure. All the information we need is there, even the timetable. There's a ferry service every day between Vienna and Passau on the German border. It stops at Dürnstein and Linz.'

James looked at his watch.

'I say!' he cried. 'Couldn't you have said so earlier? It leaves at eight o'clock! We'll barely make it!'

'Don't panic. I called reception to order a taxi. It will be downstairs in a minute and will take us to the Reichsbrücke boarding point. We'll be there in plenty of time.'

XVII

AT W— CASTLE

The *Habsburg* was one of those elegant paddle steamers which crisscross the Danube and delight the tourists, and indeed the Viennese as well.

The ferry was not very busy on a Monday morning and it was a pleasure to enjoy the view from its deserted decks. Unlike the day before, it was dry and the sun regularly broke through the low clouds.

We positioned ourselves on deckchairs at the front of the boat for observation purposes. The tall chimney exhaled a delicate wisp of black vapour. After we had left behind the village of Grinzing and Mount Leopoldsberg with its famous belvedere marking the northernmost point of Vienna, for several hours we saw only flat, sandy banks.

Shortly after eleven o'clock, the Danube, whilst still impressive, narrowed noticeably and the banks suddenly steepened to create a landscape of unparalleled magnificence, a succession of small valleys covered with orchards and forests reputed to be full of game. A member of the crew confirmed that we had just entered the Wachau valley and were, at that very moment, passing the ancient city of Krems, the first stage of our journey.

Now we had to pay attention and carefully examine each twist of the landscape.

I had taken the precaution of sketching a picture of the castle I had glimpsed in my vision on to a piece of paper for James. I had portrayed it perched on its rocky summit with the tower with the pointed roof in the foreground and, behind, a second, taller tower without a roof and connected to the first one by a wing of the building. In front of the rock, I had remembered to include the shady islet.

The advertising brochure had not exaggerated There were a plethora of ancient ruins on either side of the gorge. Over the centuries the area's tortuous geography had inspired the toughest builders. Emperors, kings, princes, tyrants and wealthy bandits had vied with one another in their audacity to build impregnable fortresses. For hours we sailed past military and religious architectural treasures: Göttweig, Stein, Dürnstein (where we docked for half an hour), Spitz and Aggstein. All of them, were surrounded by woods and vines and had their fair share of romantic castles, nearly ruined eyries, churches and monasteries.

But of my castle there was no trace! When our steamer reached the grandiose Melk Abbey in the middle of the afternoon, and a gently undulating wide plain replaced the uneven terrain of Wachau, I could not hide my disappointment.

'Are you sure you drew it right? Maybe your memory is playing tricks on you and you've forgotten an essential element?'

'No!' I protested. 'And even if that were the case, I would have done a double-take as we passed it. The truth is that it must be somewhere else.'

'Arghh! So we'll have to retrace our steps then. There's no point continuing to Passau.'

'The next stop is Linz,' I mused, consulting the brochure. 'Over forty miles from here. We'll have to wait until we get there. Then we'll take the first boat back to Vienna.'

In good spirits despite this setback, and not having eaten all day, James encouraged me to go with him to the restaurant where we sustained ourselves with a plate of beef prepared in the local style and enormous portions of *Kartoffeln*. Then we wandered up and down the deck to pass the time until we reached Linz.

It was nearly seven o'clock in the evening. The sun was about to set behind a wooded hill, blotting out the autumnal scene until the following day, when the Danube narrowed again and was squeezed between the overhanging ledges of the Bohemian Massif. The river twisted round two bends and then suddenly revealed the brooding outline of a castle with a pointed roof.

'James! James!' I cried, pointing to the stone construction which was about to disappear from sight with the last rays of the sun. 'That's it! That's the castle!'

Everything was there: the two towers, the colossal granite rock and the island that the boat was about to pass on the port side at that very moment.

'You're right! It's exactly like your drawing!'

We immediately hurried to find the captain to negotiate an impromptu landing. He was not easily convinced. His obstinacy was finally overcome when James produced a crisp bank note from his wallet.

Eventually, he gave the order to switch off the engines and a sailor lowered a skiff into the water.

Five minutes later, we landed on a bank of grey sand and the sailor and his boat returned to the *Habsburg*. A few minutes later the lights from the paddle steamer faded from the other side of the island.

Behind us, night had completely enveloped the peak and its fortress, whose threatening presence we felt even more intensely.

Above, a full moon was rising over a forest of conifers.

After the daytime splendour of the banks of the Danube, there was a sinister atmosphere, rife with the legends of Bohemia and

Moravia. At that moment we would not have been at all surprised if a raging werewolf or a vampire with incisors dripping with blood had crossed our path.

A short walk along the shore brought us to a village. We decided to go to an inn nestling outside the village on the slope of a hill to plan our next move.

The first thing I did was to request a telephone to call the reception desk at the Regina hotel in Vienna so that someone could inform Superintendent Fourier (who I believed would soon be in Vienna) of our new destination: W— Castle, near the village of Strelka.

The innkeeper and the villagers we questioned about the fortress over a glass of *Weisswein* seemed reluctant to expand on the subject. They let it be understood that it was preferable not to say anything, especially to strangers.

We did not press the issue and the son of the house, who was as unwilling to talk as the others, accompanied us to our respective rooms.

The inn was right by the castle and it offered a very advantageous view. I stood and gazed for a long time at the austere silhouette illuminated by the moon. It was exactly as I had drawn it, with its ramparts and its tall square tower, from where people must have sounded the alarm against invaders in the past. The tower with the pointed roof was on the other side and so not visible but I guessed it was similar to the square one.

After several minutes a light appeared in a window halfway up, but I only had time to make out the shape of a person before the room was in darkness again. So there was definitely someone in the *Burg*. As no other rooms were lit up, I concluded that the occupied part was in the other tower, away from people's gaze.

'Did you see the window?' exclaimed my friend, charging into the room.

'Yes.'

'It wasn't Kessling. Whoever it was looked frail, stunted ...'

'With luck, we'll get there before him. We should do – we haven't been idle since we reached Austria.'

'If we've overtaken him, we mustn't waste a second, Andrew. We should go to the castle tonight!'

'What?' I cried, alarmed at my friend's eagerness. 'Why the hurry? I'm sure Superintendent Fourier is already on his way. He'll be with us at the latest the day after tomorrow.'

'The day after tomorrow? But that's too late! We must use our advantage and find out what's going on in that damned castle. We must act tonight! We'll make a start when everyone in the inn is asleep!'

Grabbing me by the shoulders, James led me out of the room.

'Where are you taking me?'

'To eat. We must build up our strength.'

For my friend the decision had been made and it was a waste of time trying to change his mind. Anyway, maybe he was right. James was the archetypal action man; his brain was sharper and more agile when he was in danger. The opposite was true of me. Outside the silence and quiet of a reading room, where I was able to unravel the most convoluted plots, my mind felt confused and more often than not I got in a muddle when I felt threatened. All the same, we had not travelled halfway across Europe just to wait for the arrival of reinforcements. We should at least try to get some more information.

It was nearly ten o'clock. Downstairs in the dining hall the regulars were gathering. My friend ordered a plate of revolting dumpling made from bread, lard and flour, washed down with a pint of light ale. As always whenever he got a whiff of adventure, James was in good spirits. As far as I was concerned, the prospect of entering the fortress had ruined my appetite and I kept my eyes on the cuckoo clock.

Shortly after midnight, when everyone had left, we went back upstairs and waited for more than an hour in James's room while the household nodded off.

When all was quiet, my friend implored me not to move and disappeared without explanation. Ten minutes later he came back with a big smile on his face.

'The lights are out. The manager is fast asleep. We can go!'

'How do we get out of the inn without being seen?'

'This way,' he replied, opening the window. 'My room is above a shed. If we use the gutter along the front, it couldn't be easier to get down on to the roof and then jump to the ground. The shed wall is fairly low so we can come back the same way.'

James didn't give me time to reply. Without further ado, he stepped over the windowsill, landed silently on the shed roof and jumped nimbly down. Then he waved his arms to indicate that I should follow him. This was not the time to hesitate. I managed to reach the shed without too much trouble but, instead of leaping to the ground (I was nearly seven feet up after all), I grabbed a beam to slide down, which left me with scratches and a tear in my jacket, while my friend chuckled under his breath.

At two o'clock in the morning we were on the tortuous path up to the *Burg*. Access by car was impossible. The only way to reach the castle was on foot.

After a short time we came to the bottom of the ramparts. The castle, such as it was, stood on the right-hand side of the hill, directly above the Danube. It was composed of three architectural elements: the two towers which I have already mentioned and a building with a red-tiled roof which connected one to the other. Fortifications surrounded the buildings and formed a courtyard where lords of old would have gathered their troops. On both sides the walls were made of stone. There was no way of walking around the castle without risking falling down a steep drop.

Until that day I had imagined that castles of this kind were protected by a drawbridge and a thick portcullis with a deep moat preventing access. Instead of such a gothic set-up, the entrance to the *Burg* was through two wooden doors. One – admittedly high and wide but of derisory proportions compared to the fortress – opened on to the courtyard. The second, which appeared to be a simple wicket gate, provided access to the square tower.

James immediately climbed the stone steps. Having checked that the doors were locked, he came down and considered the walls carefully.

'It's impossible to get into the tower. The first window is sixteen or seventeen feet up and it has bars. But I think I can reach the lantern by the door opening on to the courtyard. If I pull myself up to the window there, I can then jump down into the courtyard.'

He peered through the keyhole.

'The courtyard is enormous. There must be a way to get into the castle through there. Anyway, the place seems deserted.'

'What about me?' I asked, disconcerted, not imagining for a moment that I could join him in his acrobatics.

'Once inside, I'll find a way to open the door for you. In the meantime, you can be my ladder!'

I hesitated before giving him a hand. There was no guarantee that James would be able to get me inside; he was taking a big risk.

'Come on, hurry! There's no other option. And nothing's going to happen to me!'

He took a small pistol out of his pocket and removed the magazine at the bottom of the barrel to show me that it was full of bullets.

'Where did you find that?'

'At the inn. While everyone was asleep I went through their drawers. It's a Mauser 1910, a semi-automatic. German soldiers used it during the war.'

Decisively, my friend pushed me against the wall under the old unlit lantern. It took all my strength not to collapse under his weight as he climbed on to my shoulders. Just when I felt it was impossible for me to hold on for much longer, James managed to grab the lantern which, happily, was firmly attached. Then he heaved himself up. He was now hanging eight feet up and the window arch was only a few feet above him. He swung his leg up to reach the window ledge. Then, judging that he had enough support, he pulled himself up so that he was sitting on the window ledge, looking down at me mockingly.

'If I'm tortured and you hear me screaming, I can count on you, can't I, Andrew? You'll call the police? With luck, you'll arrive in time to save me from certain death.'

'It's madness for you to go off into the castle on your own. Let's wait until Fourier arrives!'

Just then I heard a muffled sound as he landed in the courtyard. Through the gaps round the doorway all I could see was moonlight.

'Is everything all right?' I murmured.

'Uh, yep! I've fractured half a dozen bones but I'll be all right.'

'Can you open the damned door?'

'Sorry! It's definitely locked and I can't see any way of getting it to budge. Never mind. I'll just have a quick look round. Twenty minutes. No more, I promise!'

I cursed myself for letting James go into the *Burg* alone. It was inhabited. And everything pointed to its being the place where the unknown person who had sent the telegram found at La Toison d'Or had expressly invited Öberlin to go.

All I could do was hope that my friend came back quickly.

I went down the steps and walked a short way towards the village. From there, I could see the window in the square tower where we had glimpsed the light earlier.

The wait was interminable.

Despite his promise, James was not back after twenty minutes.

It was three o'clock in the morning and I was beside myself with anxiety. I paced up and down outside the fortress, climbing the steps at regular intervals to examine the courtyard through the keyhole, trying to spot my friend.

I had just gone down the steps again for the umpteenth time and was standing on the path when I thought I heard muffled voices below. I immediately hid behind a shrub.

Someone was coming up to the castle. I prayed that James wouldn't reappear at that very moment!

I fell to the ground and held my breath.

At the top of the path four figures appeared, walking in single file. The first was athletically built and wore a leather jacket and cap; he was closely followed by a man of average height with greying temples who was dressed in a dark coat; about six feet behind them a young woman with a scarf stuffed into her mouth and her wrists tied was being closely guarded by a man who looked enormous.

Despite the full moon I couldn't make out the features of the man in the coat but I immediately had the same uneasy feeling that I had experienced every time I became aware of the Austrian's presence. Deep down, I knew that the man who had hidden behind the mask of Andreas Eberlin, Hans-Rudolf von Öberlin and Herr Kessling was a few feet away from me.

As the group passed me, I heard the first man speak to the second in German. I didn't understand what was said but he called him Herr Professor twice.

When they reached the castle, they climbed the steps and stood in front of the wicket gate. The man in the jacket took out a torch and turned it on to help the man I supposed to be Kessling open the door. Then they entered the square tower.

As the young woman refused to follow them, the giant seized her firmly by the waist and heaved her on to his shoulder. Carrying the girl, he too entered the *Burg* and didn't close the door behind him.

I only hesitated for a few seconds. An opportunity like this wouldn't come along again and I couldn't possibly leave James to get out of such a tricky situation on his own.

I dashed out of my hiding place, went up the steps and slipped into the tower.

Their footsteps reverberated in the quiet of the night. Far away, the torchlight danced in the shadows.

I didn't want to risk bumping into anything, so I crawled to a kind of trunk and hid behind it.

The group had reached a door from which electric light spilt and for a moment I could see where I was. It was an old weapons room, completely empty apart from the trunk I was leaning against. A little further away, half a dozen cases were piled up.

After a few minutes the man in the jacket came back. The beam of his torch narrowly missed me and, luckily, he didn't see me. He closed the door to the wicket gate, locked it and disappeared again, this time leaving me in complete darkness.

I couldn't go back. Now I too was locked in the castle. I had to find James, and quickly.

I got up and struck a few matches to light my way. I put my ear up against the door at the end of the room. I couldn't hear anything so I opened the door and poked my head round.

I found myself in a kind of ante-room leading through an open door to a long passage. In the middle of the room was a table with a bottle of brandy, two half-empty glasses and two piles of playing cards. It appeared that the party had been interrupted by the appearance of Kessling and his accomplices.

Including the three who had just arrived, there were now at least five people in the fortress, not counting the young female prisoner.

What should I do now? And where was James hiding?

The group had probably gone through the passage. Relatively wide at first, it narrowed after thirty or forty feet and became a simple corridor, nine feet wide, with a series of heavy doors with locks and peepholes. Cells!

Right at the end, a red wooden door provided access to the tower with the pointed roof.

I had already gone through the door and was moving into the passage when I heard moans coming from one of the furthest cells. I could have sworn it was a woman's voice. Her groans were turning into violent cries, echoing through the old walls of the fortress.

Abruptly, the red door opened and a small man wearing a white doctor's coat came out, accompanied by Kessling and the man in the leather jacket.

I only just had time to turn round and hide in a corner.

The scraping of a bolt indicated that they were opening the cell. The cries ceased for a moment and then grew even louder before stopping again, giving way to a heavy and agonising silence.

I was about to leave my hiding place when a noise behind me made me jump. A few steps away there was a wooden door which I hadn't noticed before, providing access to the courtyard. When it rattled again it was clear that someone was trying to open it from the outside.

I had to react or it would all be over for me. As soon as Kessling's accomplice opened the door I would be discovered.

The door had already begun to open. I pressed myself up against the wall and got ready. As a sturdy-looking fellow came over the threshold, I immediately pounced. Unfortunately, I had already launched myself when I recognised the barrel of James's semi-automatic shining in the darkness. I was about to throw myself at my faithful friend. My knee smashed into his hip while my foot struck the hand holding the pistol, pressing his finger down on the trigger.

The shot rang out just as we fell on to the flagstones.

We got up at the same time, imagining that our enemies would appear from all sides. Instead of the clatter of their feet, however, we heard yet more increasingly frequent and deafening cries.

The detonation had mingled with the loud cries and seemed to have gone unnoticed.

'Good heavens, Andrew! What has got into you? You almost broke one of my ribs!'

'Sorry. I thought you were one of Kessling's men. Did you know that he's here with two of his sidekicks?'

'I thought it must be him. He didn't hang around then, the blighter!'

'Have you been able to explore the castle?'

'Only part of it. I couldn't get close to the cells. Two men were watching the corridor from a distance, playing cards. But a woman is being held, I'm sure of it.'

'Kessling came with a prisoner. It must be her we can hear.'

'No. The cries started before he arrived.'

In the corridor the captive was screaming her head off.

'It's enough to make your blood run cold!' I exclaimed. 'It sounds like she's being tortured.'

'Or—'

The screams suddenly stopped and in their place we could hear little whining sounds. Plaintive wails – like those of a newborn baby!

From the sound of voices in the passage, the three men appeared to have left the cell and were returning to the tower with the pointed roof.

With renewed energy I got up and approached the corridor.

James did the same after picking up his gun.

As I looked down the passage, the man with the cap was about to close the door. The doctor and Kessling had already gone through. In the doctor's arms I glimpsed the naked body of a newborn baby and Kessler was smiling like someone who had just done something amazing.

The words of the telegram came back to me: 'We have chosen new breeders. Confirmation birth 1 expected on 23rd. Awaiting your return to participate in great work.'

Today was 23 October as of four hours ago. These people were diabolically precise. That was when the terrifying truth dawned on me. Suddenly, I knew what the Marquis de Brindillac's incredible discovery had been and the secret behind Herr Kessling's elaborate, absurd and insane enterprise.

A shiver ran down my spine, and my fear intensified as I felt a sudden pressure against the back of my head. I was right to be alarmed. When I turned round, I found a blond man with a face covered in scars waving a pistol under my nose. Next to me, James had his hands on his head and was being threatened with a semi-automatic.

The sidekick, who had a shaved head and sharply pointed ears, barked at me savagely: '*Hände hoch! Schnell!*'

I obeyed and put my hands up.

James's pistol was now tucked into the guard's belt.

XVIII

THE MASTER RACE IS BATTERY-FARMED

The two men pointed to the corridor. In silence we walked past the cells to the door through which Kessling and his accomplices had disappeared.

The man with pointed ears knocked on the door.

'*Gehen Sie hinein!*' replied a voice.

The door opened. I was pushed through first.

We entered a room which was only partly furnished. An old couch and coloured leather chairs were arranged in a semicircle in front of a fireplace with a blazing fire.

On either side of the hearth were shelves filled with leather-bound books. Elsewhere, coats of arms covered the walls – probably dating from the days when the castle had been an ancestral home.

Above the couch a ceiling lamp provided dim light, barely supplemented by two antique chandeliers and a crystal lamp. On the right a stone staircase led to the upper floors. The rest of the room was in semi-darkness.

The athletic-looking man, who had put his leather jacket and cap on the back of a chair, was leaning against the mantelpiece with a glass in his hand. He watched us enter without saying a word or showing any surprise.

Opposite him, with his back to us, sat Kessling, his hair visible above a large yellow leather armchair. A thick cloud of smoke floated above his head.

The man in the white coat and the newborn baby were not there.

185

'Ah! Mr Singleton, Mr Trelawney! We were expecting you. But please, do come in!'

The invitation was given in perfect English.

James and I exchanged disconcerted looks.

Our host was leaning over the arm of his chair and, for the first time, I could see him properly. He was about fifty-five with black hair streaked with silver and brushed back. He had a square face, a strong jaw and a high forehead which attested to a proud and determined temperament, but it was not a particularly remarkable face apart from the eyes! Oh, those eyes! What eyes! So dark, so black, so deep! The most intense eyes I had ever seen and, above them, a pair of eyebrows shaped like circumflexes.

And yet, the person in front of me was not a stranger. I recognised the shape of his head and the proportions of his features. Was it because I had tried to picture his face so many times over the last few days?

'Andrew!' murmured my friend. 'I know this fellow!'

'Aha!' roared Kessling, getting up from his chair. 'But yes, my friend! You are right, we have already met.'

He was dressed in an elegant grey wool suit and he seemed eminently respectable with his black tie and shiny shoes.

'I had longer hair and splendid glasses with tinted lenses,' he encouraged us, observing our confusion. 'The theatre is my great unfulfilled passion. It is a compulsion. I have to dress up and change the way I look and speak.'

'The musician!' exclaimed James. 'At the Café de la Place Blanche!'

'Impossible!' I cried. 'The goatee was real. Otherwise, I would have pulled it off!'

Kessling approached us, clapping his hands. He was delighted with the effect he had had.

'Bravo, Mr Trelawney, bravo! The secret is in the glue. The one use was invented by an old make-up artist from the Burgtheatre in Vienna. He created it for Christian-Dietrich Meyerinck at the start of his career. The actor suffered from excessive sweating and his hairpieces had the unfortunate habit of coming unstuck in the middle of a show at the most dramatic moment. Imagine the audience's hilarity! Happily, thanks to this very effective glue, he has been able to play all the classical roles and is internationally renowned. A mixture of lemon water and bicarbonate of soda is all that is required to remove the effects of the glue.'

He went to draw on his cigar but it had gone out. He flicked his lighter and played with the flame, studying us.

'How did you know that we were in the castle?' asked my friend.

'You followed me on to the Orient Express. There was no reason to think you wouldn't find out where I was hiding. It was a question of knowing when. I admit that you have been even faster than I expected. When Franz over there went back earlier to lock the tower, he caught a glimpse of someone in the light of his torch. Of course, he didn't react. It was more amusing that way. But don't stand on ceremony, gentlemen. Sit down!'

The two brutes behind us pressed the barrels of their weapons into our backs.

'Georg! Josef! Be polite, please. Ah, my friends, please excuse their manners which are a little uncouth. But they are loyal.'

We moved forward and sat on the couch.

'Why did you try to kill André Breton, Herr Kessling?' I asked. 'Or should I use another name for you?'

'That one is fine. Or, even better, do me the pleasure of calling me Johannes.'

'So what reason did you have to kill Breton? Despite his interest in sleep and dreams, he had not entered into contact with the spirits of nature.'

'That is true, or at least not yet. But those Surrealists are always to be feared. By eliminating their leader, the entire movement would have been reduced to nothing in one go.'

'In that case, why did you not repeat your attempt?'

'Because an adversary appeared that I was not expecting, one who was a match for me, clever and perceptive.'

Kessling inclined his head in my direction as he spoke.

'When I saw you at the Café de la Place Blanche, Mr Singleton, with your pale face and dark circles under your eyes, I understood that the gates of sleep had been opened for you. Those who cross that line wear it clearly on their faces. No one knows why!'

'And so you thought you had to kill me? Because it was you in the Orient Express wasn't it, that revolting creature which almost strangled me?'

'Kill you? I never dreamt of such a thing, Mr Singleton! I just wanted to give you a good fright. On the contrary, my greatest wish was for you to join me in this obscure place so that I could present you with the fruits of my research. That is the least I could do to honour your intelligence! Then the time will come to give you the *coup de grâce*, you and your friend.'

'Your research?' enquired James, pretending not to notice the threat. 'Can you be a little clearer?'

'I would call it the most scandalous of enterprises,' I said. 'Remember, James, the book we found under the Marquis's bed at Château B——?'

The Austrian was delighted. He listened to us placidly, blowing smoke rings up to the ceiling.

'*Le Comte de Gabalis?*'

'Yes. The author reveals that amorous alliances between men and ethereal creatures can bear fruit, can create children who look human but whose mind, ingenuity and physical powers are phenomenal. If such immaterial unions were possible, the instigator of that birth would have a priceless asset at his fingertips.'

'Are you saying,' exclaimed James, 'that what we heard earlier—'

'Yes,' I replied. 'A child born of a woman and an elemental spirit.'

Kessling stubbed out his cigar and turned to me.

'One asset? Only one? Ha! You are very shrewd, my boy, but you still lack that vital spark. Appetite, by Jove! Ambition! Singleton, believe me, it is not just one I seek to create, it is a squadron, a battalion, an entire army of true masters!'

I glanced at James. He appeared to be as stunned as I was.

'In a few weeks' time,' Kessling went on, 'I intend to inseminate a large number of female elementals. At the same time, their males will impregnate the human females I have chosen. I have had one transported to the castle. Tonight, I will summon a virile representative of the elemental people to the top of the tower and order this holy union. You shall witness the marriage. It is time to begin the reproductive programme on a vast scale!'

This man was a monster.

Franz had left the fireplace and was sprawled on one of the chairs, his legs stretched out in front of him.

Georg and Josef were still in their places, halfway between their leader's chair and the door, making escape into the corridor impossible.

Behind us, the stairs offered a way out but what could we have done once we got up there? Kessling would have taken care to lock all the exits of the *Burg*. And, of course, the group was not complete. The man in the white coat and the huge man in charge of the prisoner on the path were missing. No doubt the doctor was looking after the infant but what was the other one doing? Guarding the future bride?

The best thing we could do was try to gain some time.

'You say, Herr Kessling, that you have learnt to make these

ethereal peoples submit to your ambitions. In that case, why did you not send one of them to me on the Orient Express? It would have been less dangerous than spiriting yourself into my sleep. I have read in books on magic that such psychic journeys are very risky.'

'Oh that! You have no idea how unpredictable elementals are! They may be our equals in terms of cunning and even knowledge, but they are skittish and bossy, very often lacking in moral sense. Anyone who tries to control them must take care that the servant does not turn against his master because then it would all be over for him. That is why I only have moderate confidence in their kind. I much prefer their human offspring. By mating with our males and our females, these invisible spirits give birth to beings which, as the great magicians discovered, naturally and instinctively obey. For now, operations which require – how can I put it – a certain finesse, well, I like to do them myself!'

Kessling looked at his watch and then ordered Franz to go and find someone called Bernhard at the top of the tower.

'Five o'clock in the morning already!' announced Kessling, rising. 'In a little over two hours daybreak will be here. I want the second member of my future army to be conceived tonight, the same night as the first was born. Like me, you know how important symbols are.'

After a pause, the henchman reappeared at the bottom of the stairs.

'*Sie fest schläft!*' he announced.

'*Wunderbar!*'

The Austrian's face was radiant.

'The bride is sleeping like an angel. I will be able to proceed with the invocation. Follow me, my friends. It is time to go to the marriage bed. I'm sure you're dying to see for yourselves.'

Kessling went up the stairs, followed by Franz who had taken the precaution of picking up an oil lamp. James and I, still at the mercy of Georg and Josef's pistols, fell in behind them.

We followed them until they reached the top of the tower and a door guarded by the giant – Bernhard no doubt. He was slouched on a chair which threatened to break at any moment, his arms resting on a table where a candle was burning. He was even more enormous than I had thought.

The door had a peephole like the cells in the passage.

The landing was ridiculously small and we could not all fit on it at once. One of Kessling's men, Josef or Georg, I don't know which, was still standing on the top step.

It was a strange place for a marital bedroom. No doubt Kessling had chosen it because it was right at the top of the castle, within reach of the sky. Symbols again. The other tower was actually taller by at least thirty feet but it was also closer to the village. Here, overlooking the Danube, there was no one to hear any screams.

'Gentlemen, I am going to enter this room and begin the invocation. It is not the only method to contact a representative of the elemental spirits. Another is to pass through the gates of sleep oneself to gain access to the invisible kingdom. There, with experience and great psychic strength, one can force a spirit to accomplish marvels. But, in the circumstances, it is better to conjure one up.'

Kessling indicated that Bernhard should open the door. He took an enormous key out of his trouser pocket and inserted it into the lock.

'I advise you not to miss any of the ceremony,' added Kessling, pointing to the small opening in the door before it closed behind him.

It was out of the question that I should approach the peephole. But James, despite my exhortations, couldn't stop himself putting his eye up to the wire mesh.

Bernhard had sat down again. The key had not been returned to his pocket but was lying on the table near Franz's oil lamp.

Franz kept eyeing us suspiciously.

'Kessling is standing in the middle of the room,' murmured my friend. 'There's a large four-poster bed at the end. I can't see very well, there isn't much light, but I can see the shape of a body. It must be the prisoner.'

James was silent for a few seconds and then resumed his commentary.

'It's strange. Now my eyes are used to the darkness, I think I can make out a large pattern on the floor in front of Kessling. A sort of star with five points.'

'The pentagram or Flamboyant Star,' I replied. 'The traditional symbol of the domination of the spirit over the elements. By drawing that star thaumaturgists enslaved creatures of the air, fire, water and earth in order to force them to submit.'

This time James remained silent for a long time, taxing my nerves.

In the end, I could take it no longer.

'What is he doing now?'

'He's chanting but I can't understand what he's saying.'

At that moment Kessling must have moved on to a new stage of his invocation because I could suddenly hear his voice loudly reciting a prayer in Latin.

'Now he's really bellowing!' exclaimed James. 'But the sleeping woman is still not waking up.'

'She is imprisoned in her sleep under the control of the incubus.'

My friend turned from the peephole to look at me.

'We can't let him do this, Andrew!'

Bernhard was still sitting on his chair. On my left Franz was looking us up and down with a sly smile. Behind us Josef and Georg were standing on the edge of the landing, their pistols at the ready.

Suddenly hurried footsteps could be heard coming up the stairs. Whoever it was must have important news to impart. Before he appeared at the top of the tower I heard him wheezing and he had to stop several times to get his breath back. At last, the man in the white coat made his way past Georg and Josef and stood in front of Franz, hands on hips, gasping.

'*Polizei! Polizei! Überall um die Burg!*'

'*Polizei? Was erzählst du denn da?*'

The police! They had surrounded the castle! So good old Fourier had got my message and hurried to find us.

Franz took the doctor by the shoulder and, after ordering the other two to stay where they were, ushered him towards the stairs. Clearly, he wanted to judge the situation for himself before warning his boss and risking interrupting the rite.

After they had disappeared Georg and Josef wavered slightly. They didn't know what to do now and only one (the one with the pockmarked skin) continued to point his pistol in our direction.

That was the moment my friend chose to act. He suddenly rushed at them. Unable to avoid his charge, they fell backwards and tumbled down the stairs with a terrible crash. While he recovered his pistol from the belt of one of the crooks, James shouted at me to take care of Bernhard.

Take care of Bernhard! And how was I supposed to do that? The man, who was three times my size, had not been slow to react. Luckily, flexibility was not his strong point. As he went to grab me by the throat, I rolled between his legs and hit the table.

I grabbed the lamp and the metal key in one move and hurried into the bedroom where my friend joined me after giving Bernhard a fatal blow to the head. I locked the door behind him.

Kessling turned round as we entered, his eyes full of violence and rage. He took up his position again in front of the pentagram and fixed his attention on the four-poster bed where the young woman, unclothed, lay sleeping.

'There's no more an infernal creature in here than at Piccadilly Circus at midday!' mocked James.

'Be quiet, you imbecile!' thundered Kessling without shifting his gaze from the sleeping woman. 'We can't see it, that's all. But the spirit is here, moving around above her. And I can confirm that the bride is to his taste!'

James seized the oil lamp I was holding and moved towards the bed. Kessling grabbed my friend by the arm and forced him back.

'I order you not to enter the area beyond the sacred star. It alone protects us from demons and their unpredictable reactions.'

My friend stopped immediately.

'The spirit cannot do anything to us, James! He can only act through sleep. We have nothing to fear.'

'Here he is!' cried Kessling. 'The holy union is finally going to begin! A second master will be born from this magical night!'

On the bed the young woman appeared to be having a convulsion. Her eyelids fluttered slightly and her body began to jolt. At first it looked like the jerky movements I had noticed in my friend but, very quickly, her spasms took on a worrying intensity. Her stomach was crushed under the weight of something that could not be seen. She was moaning terribly and writhing ever more violently.

Ignoring the Austrian's advice, James placed the lamp at the foot of the four-poster and rushed towards the sleeping woman. I did likewise, making my way to the other side of the bed.

After a few moments' hesitation, Kessling crossed the line that he himself had fixed and hurried towards us.

'Stop, you ignoramuses! What are you doing?'

James shoved him back, sending him reeling to the other side of the room.

Then, as we had done for André Breton in his studio, we used all our energy to try to rouse the woman from her sleep and bring her back to consciousness. But this time a colossal force appeared to be opposing us and held her firmly in a trance-like state.

'Let that woman go or it will cost you your life!'

Kessling had risen and was getting ready to throw himself at us again but in his hurry he knocked over the lamp that was on the floor. The glass broke and the oil spread to the sheets of the four-poster which caught fire.

This accident was a godsend for us. The flames seemed to have an immediate effect on our invisible adversary because, in an instant, it became evident that the sleeping woman had been delivered from the dream which had possessed her. Responding to our calls, she opened her eyes. Her lips moved in an effort to speak but the poor woman was in a state of shock.

James tore down part of the bed canopy and used it to cover her nakedness. Then he lifted the young woman up just before the fire, growing more intense by the second, reached the mattress.

'What should we do with him?' I asked, pointing to Kessling, who was lying on the floor, uttering a crazy litany of hate-filled imprecations.

'Leave him to his miserable fate!'

The flames were now licking at the wooden beams. In a few moments they would reach the roof. We had to get out of this part of the *Burg* as quickly as possible. I opened the door with the key and turned it twice in the keyhole behind me.

James was right. The villain was going to get what he deserved.

We stepped over Bernhard's body and the twisted limbs of Georg and Josef on the stairs and then ran as quickly as we could. In my friend's arms the young woman was struggling to regain consciousness.

When we reached a landing we heard sharp cries coming from the room below. James pointed to a door.

'That leads to the first floor of the central building, above the cells. I think we should go that way to reach the square tower. Franz and the doctor don't seem to be able to agree on what to do. Let's try and avoid them!'

I pushed open the door and we ran down a long shadowy corridor. As we left the marital bedroom, I had automatically picked up Bernhard's candle. I therefore led the way, holding the candlestick out in front of me.

At the end of the corridor another door led to a relatively spacious room which was lit by an overhead electric light. On the table was a full medical kit, including some items which had been displaced (syringes, percussion hammer, stethoscope, height gauge, scales). Above, the shelves were filled with pillboxes and glass bottles.

James put the woman down in an armchair. Her face was dreadfully pale.

From the open window we could see the hill and the grey roofs of the nearest houses in Strelka shining in the bright night.

Below, about fifty police officers in uniform, armed to the teeth, were massed in front of the castle.

On the steps, I recognised the tweed suit and bowler hat of Superintendent Fourier. Three men were at his side: Jacques Lacroix was one and Raymond Dupuytren another. I could not identify the last.

Nearby, a fellow in a trench coat was positioning his men. On the path, villagers had gathered behind a row of policemen, alerted by the flames.

I leant out of the window and shouted to the superintendent, waving my arms.

'Singleton! Thank heavens! You're safe!' he cried jubilantly when he saw me.

'Yes, Superintendent! Fire broke out at the back of the castle. There are only two who are still a threat. The others can't do us any harm. A woman is being held prisoner in one of the cells. We have another young lady with us who needs help. And there's a baby too! Come quickly!'

'A what?'

The man in the trench coat gave the order to go in. A battering ram struck the wicket gate of the square tower and another broke down the entrance to the courtyard. As soon as the first police officers entered the *Burg*, shots rang out but the exchange of fire only lasted five minutes. Suddenly, it stopped and we heard steps on the stairs.

A door opened. Fourier, Lacroix and Dupuytren burst in to congratulate us. Behind them, I recognised the pretty face of Mademoiselle de Brindillac, her head covered by a shawl.

Amélie, the perfect Samaritan, moved towards the young woman we had just rescued from the realm of sleep and, taking her grey woollen coat from her shoulders, she helped the young woman to put it on.

The man in the trench coat appeared in the doorway. An imperial moustache spread like the wings of a parrot under his long red nose.

'Singleton! Trelawney! Let me introduce Baron Sedlinsky, Vienna's chief of police. It is thanks to the Baron that so many of us were able to get here.'

'Thank you, Baron! My word,' I continued, addressing the superintendent, 'you didn't waste any time, did you? Did the French government dip into public funds to charter a special plane?'

'You are not far from the truth, my friend. The Interior Minister authorised the use of one of his planes. We took off from Le Bourget airport at sunrise and at one o'clock in the afternoon we were in Vienna. The receptionist at the Regina told me where you had gone:

W— Castle. Unfortunately, it took us time to find a car to get here. But, by the way, can someone tell me what's happened to Öberlin?'

'Kessling,' James corrected. 'That's his latest identity. He is locked in the south-west tower. Unarmed and harmless. When we left, the flames of hell were about to roast him.'

An Austrian inspector entered the room and exchanged a few words with Baron Sedlinsky.

'Gentlemen! The fire is spreading!' Vienna's chief of police declared in French. 'We cannot stop it. We must leave immediately.'

'Good heavens! The baby!' I cried. 'We must find it and quickly.'

'What is all this about a —'

'Listen!' said Amélie.

We all listened but could only hear the commotion on the ground floor.

'Listen' she repeated. 'It's like someone moaning.'

Indeed, we could make out a kind of vague sigh, a far-off breathing and slight hissing which seemed to be coming from behind a curtain.

'That's him. That's the baby,' I cried, rushing behind the table.

Pulling aside the velvet curtain, I discovered a narrow room where a dozen cradles were lined up. It was a nursery, rudimentary and lacking basic modern comforts but adequate no doubt for babies possessed of exceptional life force.

I approached one of the beds. Inside, a baby was sleeping.

The others came forward cautiously. At my side, Amélie let out a gasp of surprise.

'My goodness, it's true! Poor little thing.'

She picked up the newborn baby who opened his blue-green eyes and gazed at her.

A few minutes later, before the sun came up, we were walking along the path which would take us away from W— Castle for ever, leaving behind us the sad spectacle of flames engulfing the roof of the central building.

EPILOGUE

For us the case was finally closed. Johannes Kessling had perished in the castle fire and an explanation for the murders of the various sleep specialists over the last few months had been found, incredible as it was.

In the car back to Vienna, I told Superintendent Fourier about the latest turn of events, not forgetting the presumed supernatural origins of the newborn child. What were we supposed to think of that infant now in Amélie's care in the car behind us? Would he really develop mythical powers? Was that not just the delirious fantasy of Herr Professor? What proof did we have that he was not the offspring of two completely ordinary human beings?

Moreover, we had no witnesses to reveal the identity of his father. The mother had been found lying in her cell, having bled to death. As for Franz and the doctor, they had seen the game was up and thrown themselves in front of the police bullets.

My stories of supernatural unions left Superintendent Fourier sceptical to say the least. I did manage to persuade him though that it would not be prudent to entrust the infant to the Austrian regime. The best thing would be to place him under the protection of the French state so that doctors could follow his development day by day and assess his real faculties as soon as possible.

When we reached the capital Fourier negotiated with Baron Sedlinsky in order to obtain his authorisation to take the newborn baby with us, which he managed to do without too much difficulty. It goes without saying that Vienna's chief of police had been told the bare minimum about Kessling's odious plan and that no mention was made of the possible nature of the baby.

In the early afternoon I made a detour to the Regina[17] to pick up my bag. An hour later Fourier, Lacroix, Mademoiselle de Brindillac, Dupuytren, James and I took our seats with the baby on board the plane chartered by the Interior Minister. During the flight Amélie and Jacques suggested giving the baby a name so the boy was christened Auguste, in memory of the Marquis whose funeral had been held on Sunday at Étampes cemetery.

In the evening, the Blériot landed at Le Bourget airport and, as midnight struck, I returned to my room at the Hôtel Saint-Merri which I had left three days previously in great haste.

Although I was exhausted from my journey, I only managed to doze off as the sun began to rise. For the last few days I had been living in a kind of waking dream. The line between my real life and my dream life had become increasingly blurred. Now the time had come for me to return to a more solid, tangible existence. Already, the gates of sleep had closed for ever. Perhaps in a few weeks' time I would wonder if I had imagined the whole thing?

When I awoke I had to accept that my stranger from the steamer had not visited me. I had so wanted to see her one last time! She was the one who had helped me to see the light in this investigation. She was the one, above all, to whom I owed my life.

She didn't visit me that night or the following night or any other night. So what was I to think? Hadn't Kessling himself stressed the inconstant and unpredictable nature of elemental entities? I had been chosen by her to foil a wicked plan which threatened the balance between the worlds. With that mission now fulfilled, had my stranger turned away from me?

The mystery remained but that did not stop me recording my dreams. In fact, it was my dream diary which led to my success in the difficult Brussels Vampire case.

Of course, every time I have looked back on what happened in Paris (and even now as I write these words), I have had to admit that a tiny part of me, the conservative, logical and rational part, has always maintained that the stranger from the steamer was a product of my imagination, a creature I had invented in my overactive subconsciousness. However, deep down I know that the truth is otherwise. The events recorded here are proof enough of that.

My investigation into the death of Nerval had not moved forward. Nonetheless, James and I agreed to take the train to London on Thursday after a well-deserved day of rest wandering through the City of Light.

At twenty minutes to midday on 25 October 1934 a taxi delivered us to the Gare du Nord. At the end of the platform, in front of the *Flèche d'Or*, Superintendent Fourier, Lacroix and Mademoiselle de Brindillac were waiting with happy smiles to bid us farewell.

Fourier took the opportunity to pass on the President's official thanks; Jacques and Amélie announced the date of their wedding.

After many warm words, the whistle blew. As I mounted the step of the carriage, Lacroix held out a leather case.

'What's this?'

'Do you remember that conversation we had on Friday in the hotel lobby about the death of Gérard de Nerval?'

'Of course! You tried to bamboozle me with a story of a strange character at the top of Tour Saint-Jacques who was supposed to have been part of the investigation in 1855.'

'It wasn't a hoax, trust me! I told you that the man had given me a document and that if we were successful in our case I would show it to you. Well, here it is!'[17]

'Oh, but …'

'I offer it to you as a gift. You are without doubt the person best qualified to recognise its true significance. I will only add one thing: you have never read anything like it!'

'Ha! That is exactly what our friend the superintendent said to

202

convince me to help him in the Deadly Sleep case. I hope this won't launch me into a similar adventure.'

'You'll see! Goodbye, gentlemen! Amélie and I wish you an excellent trip! And don't forget that we are counting on your presence at our wedding!'

For now I will say nothing of the content of that mysterious manuscript. All I can say is that Lacroix had not been exaggerating and its value is indeed incalculable[18].

The train left at midday exactly and at twenty-five past three our steamer set sail from the port of Calais on an unseasonably balmy day for the end of October.

We didn't have the opportunity to return to the beautiful country of France until the end of 1935 as the curious outcome of the case of the Gargoyle with Eyes of Blood prevented us from attending our friends' marriage. However, we stayed in touch with them, as we did with dear Breton and I pride myself on the part I played in promoting his work in England and the United States. A few months after this case, an informal Surrealist group was even set up in London, to the great pride of the French writer and his followers.

As for baby Auguste, he is a young man now, and my word, he's a strapping lad. We regularly have news of him via Chief Superintendent Fourier and Lacroix who now runs the newspaper *L'Épopée*. He demonstrates surprising intellectual ability for his age and his teachers predict that he will be admitted to the prestigious Academy of Sciences or Medicine. Of course, people will say that this precocity proves nothing about the alleged wonder of his birth – unless all the members of those venerable bodies are of immaterial parentage. But let's wait a few years. There may be more surprises to come!

Finally, I must conclude on a more worrying note.

On the morning of Saturday 3 November 1934, a little over a

week after our return from France, we received a telegram from the Sûreté Nationale which threw us into turmoil. Superintendent Fourier informed us that Baron Sedlinsky's men had gone through the rubble of W— Castle and had discovered the charred bodies of Georg, Josef and Bernhard but had found no trace of a fourth body, either in the infamous tower bedroom or anywhere else in the *Burg*.

So what had become of Johannes Kessling? Had the monster managed to escape? A conjuring trick? Black magic? Joint efforts by the Sûreté Nationale and the Vienna police to dig up information on this shady character's past also proved fruitless. Kessling seemed to have landed on earth as mysteriously as he had disappeared off the face of it.

A few months later, we were informed by an agent of the British secret services that a castle in the forest of Teutberg, near Paderborn in Westphalia – Wewelsburg – had been taken over under personal orders from Hitler and turned into ceremonial headquarters for the SS, a magical stronghold for the famous Black Order, the regime's parallel army. By amazing coincidence, the establishment of Wewelsburg more or less tallied with the date of Johannes Kessling's disappearance from W— Castle.

In truth, all the indications are that Johannes Kessling did not die on 23 October 1934 on the banks of the Danube and that he and the SS-Obersturmbannführer Otto Walther von Küchlin, pursued by James and me in the winter of 1944, were one and the same person. Having given up on the idea of a battery farm for the master race, he had thrown himself into a new and terrifying enterprise.

But that is another unlikely story for another day.

A.S., 29 July

NOTES

1 *The Baker Street Phantom* - Gallic Books

2 *Gérard de Nerval, le poète et l'homme* by Aristide Marie, published by Hachette in 1914. Singleton devoured this biography, the first truly complete account of the French writer's life. (Publisher's note)

3 Built in 1862, the Théâtre des Nations changed its name to Théâtre Sarah-Bernhardt in 1949 before being renamed Théâtre de la Ville in 1967. (Publisher's note)

4 This is reported in Chapter XIV of Aristide Marie's book. Nerval was the subject of a book by Eugène de Mirecourt which had been dedicated to him in cabbalistic letters and, under a sketch, had written 'I am the other'. (Publisher's note)

5 Juve was the ingenious policeman who hunted Fantômas in the series of the same name written by Pierre Souvestre and Marcel Allain between 1911 and 1913. Tirauclair was the hero of *L'Affaire Lerouge* (1866) by Émile Geboriau. Chantecoq was one of the characters in *Belphégor* by Arthur Bernède, published in 1927. (Publisher's note)

6 In fact, different police forces coexisted in France, created according to need and without any coordination between them. In particular, a war was raging between the Sûreté Générale (which became the Sûreté Nationale in 1934), which had been autonomous since 1877 and was directly attached to the Ministry of the Interior, and the Préfecture de Police in Paris. (Publisher's note)

7 The Stavisky affair, which had come to light in December 1933, was still on everyone's minds. Denounced by the press, the scandal of false credit bonds at Crédit Municipal in Bayonne had led to the fall of the Chautemps government. The investigation had revealed numerous fraudulent relationships between the police, the justice system and politicians. (Publisher's note)

8 On 9 October, the Minister for Foreign Affairs, Louis Barthou, was killed in an attack committed by a Croatian nationalist organisation, along with King Alexander I of Yugoslavia, whom he had gone to welcome at the port of Marseille. There was an immediate debate about failings in the police protection provided for such a high-risk visit. (Publisher's note)

9 Charles Richet (1850–1935), a member of the Académie de Médecine, Nobel Prize winner in physiology and member of the Académie des Sciences, founded the Institut Métapsychique International (IMI) with Jean Meyer, Gustave Geley and Rocco Santoliquido. He was the Institut's president from 1930 until his death. (Publisher's note)

10 After the tragic death of Dr Geley in 1924, Dr Eugène Osty (1874–1938) replaced him as director of the Institut Métapsychique. (Publisher's note)

11 From the first centuries of the Middle Ages until the Inquisition, the subject fascinated everyone. The Church Fathers had admitted the existence of such creatures and the question of whether or not children could be born from supernatural unions was debated before emperors and doctors of theology. (Publisher's note)

12 Louis Aragon in *Entrée des succubes*; Robert Desnos in *Journal d'une apparition*; Max Ernst in *Visions de demi-sommeil*. (Publisher's note)

13 It would appear that Monsieur de Vallemont is referring to *Rêves et hallucinations* published by Vigot Frères in 1925. (Publisher's note)

14 It was only in the second half of the twentieth century that this was studied in more depth under the name sleep paralysis. (Publisher's note)

15 Strangely, Fritz Lang was not credited on the Boulevard de Magenta poster. I only realised that it was the French version of *The Testament of Dr Mabuse* when I saw the opening credits. It had been filmed in parallel with the original, in the same setting but with different actors, apart from the main role. The German film was banned by the Nazi regime before its release in March 1933. (Author's note)

16 Although in their time Lucretius, Aristotle and others described the jerky kind of movements seen during sleep, it was not until the development of electro-encephalographic recordings that the so-called 'paradoxical sleep' phase, a particular period of dream activity which occurs at regular intervals during sleep, was brought to light. (Author's note)

17 Shortly after his exile to London, I had the great honour of talking to Professor Sigmund Freud in connection with the sensational case of the Butterfly Man. From him I learnt that the Regina was less than five hundred yards from his former home at 19 Bergasse and that the hotel was used by a number of his overseas patients. If I

had been strolling near the entrance of the Votivkirche in the early evening in that autumn of 1934 I might have bumped into the great man. (Author's note)

18 When we were correcting the proofs of *The Dream Killer of Paris*, we received a short manuscript from William H. Barnett which had also been found in his late father's trunk. According to Mr Barnett, it is highly likely that it was the document Andrew Fowler Singleton refers to here. After consultation with the editorial committee, we sent it to a recognised expert in the authentication and dating of manuscripts. As soon as the results are known, and if they show conclusively the provenance of that text, we will immediately bring it to the public's attention. (Publisher's note)